After

N M McIntyre

@2024 by N M McIntyre

All rights reserved. No part of this publication may be reproduced, stored in a retrieval system, or transmitted, in any form or by any means, without the prior written permission of the author. Edited by Linda Nagle.

ISBN: 9798878558938
Imprint: Independently published

Facebook: N M McIntyre, Author
Instagram: n_m_mcintyre

This book is dedicated to my family & friends who have always been there for me.

When the wild sky forces storm clouds, when the frost covers the earth, when darkness threatens your light.

Be brave, & know you are loved.

Rainbows for Dad
Love for you all

After

Northern England - Present Day

I watch my breath as it materialises into the frozen air, vapour swirling away into nothingness as I pass through it, my walking boots crunching over the thin layer of ice on the tarmac path. I listen to the morning chorus, and the silence beyond this. Every so often a noise distracts from the quietness and I whip my head around at every rustle, but it is never anything more than the birds jostling for position along the tree line as they watch me with beady eyes.
I walk this way out of habit, but also because I feel safer here. Vehicles cannot access this road anymore, and you would need some kind of machine to cut free the giant chain that binds the main gates of the quarry. The fence, however, is climbable, and even if it takes a little longer to reach town this way, the route is worth the detour. As I walk, I focus on the sides of the road, just in case. There's a wild world of thick, reaching blackberry bushes looking to ensnare you if you get too close, and the dark shadows of the woodland undergrowth hiding the creatures that only come out at night. Every so

often, a deer or rabbit will startle me and race out, making me jump, disturbing the peace; but it's a perfect, welcome distraction, and no matter how frightened or alone I feel, I know the animals are here. I also know by now that this means there's no danger.

The only section of this long quarry road I don't like is the railway bridge. I am approaching it now and I already feel myself hesitating. It makes me feel uncomfortable, forcing memories that rip and tear into my heart. My stomach tightens. There are two concrete walls running parallel on either side over the tracks, and on one end of the bridge—the end closest to me—is a rusty, burned-out security van. The bonnet was mangled and compressed after hitting the wall, and inside the van sits the decomposing remains of its driver. I imagine they probably had their legs trapped by the crash and hadn't been able to get out when the flames engulfed the van, and by the time they died, help didn't exist anyway. The untouched, blackened remains are a testimony to this. I drop my head as I walk by, trying not to look at the scene, or glance at the opposite side of the wall, but I can't help myself. Faded now, etched in spray paint from the riot days, but still clear to read, is a simple graffiti motif.

There's a crude image of a needle filled with blood, and the simple text: 'VACCINE = DEATH'.

There's a second tensing of my muscles as unwelcome memories return, and I close my eyes tight to squeeze away the images that come in waves along with the feeling of terrible helplessness.

'Breathe, Elle,' I tell myself, pushing away the loud chatter, replacing it with what I am thankful for: blue skies, the sunlight, and that plastic box I found, full of dried pasta. I am alive. I am alive. I exhale, feeling slightly calmer. I'm still getting panic attacks, but I'm handling them better and better these days. I think being outside helps, surrounded by nature. I leave the bridge and the memories behind, glancing one last time at the graffiti. Funny how vaccines never really mattered in the end.

Up ahead, there's a point where I exit the quarry road and slip through a broken wire fence, I can see it from here. A popular short-cut long before the epidemic. The grass passageway is still worn down from years of footfall, and I bend through the hole to follow the winding path along the overgrown fields and hills and up towards the edge of our town, which sits proudly on a hilltop. Eventually, the path brings me out behind an old factory, and it's a short walk to the high street. Again, another point to turn my head and avert my eyes as I pass what remains of the community centre. Like the graffiti symbol, it holds terrible memories of this last year. Everything is silent.

I see a few pheasants running across the roads. There's no sign of people, and I tentatively head towards what was the main throng. *It was always a strange place, this town*, I think, a lost little place that years ago used to consist of a thriving market, with lots of fresh bakeries; a real, authentic cheesemonger that brought in the tourists; and a few butchers' shops. There was also a beautiful little coffee shop, where I would always get a bun from as a child, but when they built the industrial estate and the new-build houses at the bottom of town, all that changed. It became a weird clash of contemporary and timeworn. New supermarkets and petrol stations were created, and modernisation pushed away the people who had lived for generations in our area. I am glad my village, although rural, had been pretty isolated from all the changes in town these last ten years, but now, I guess, nothing will be changing again any time soon.

The high street is like a car crash. I step carefully over the mountain of broken glass that litters scorched paving stones, burned-out cars, broken shutters, and shattered windows. I hate coming here, but I'd like to find what I came looking for, and any other useful commodities whilst I'm here, so I make a start. The old pharmacy first, which had its shutters ripped right off its windows, is completely stripped bare, but I peer inside anyway. Instantly, I know someone has been here recently, because when I browsed inside last month there was a box of plastic combs scattered over the floor, and they're not here now. Although I can't think what use plastic combs could be to anyone. I sigh and turn my head towards the high street. The newer pharmacy at the bottom isn't an option. The army cleared it all out, and then riots saw it burn afterwards, but I guess I still have rooms and places to search that I've never investigated. There are two supermarkets, a few smaller shops, and some local boutiques. If all else fails, I will have to start looking in the houses. I could have never imagined that finding sanitary products would be such an issue.

I go from place to place quietly, disturbing the dust that has settled in the gloom of the vacant buildings, stepping gently over bust doors, plasterboard from collapsed ceilings and walls, and glass. So much glass. It's like navigating through a serial killer's funhouse, and time creeps by. I'm guessing it takes me around two hours to do a quick search of each accessible store in town, and I'm literally in and out within minutes: scan, search, scan, search, of each shelf and crevice. In one building, I notice something wedged under some of the debris. To my dismay, I pick up a green spray-bottle of air freshener. 'Damn it!'

I thought it was a Sprite or a Mountain Dew. *'Alpine Goodness'* it calls itself, and I roll my eyes. Some good it will do me. Afraid I've completely wasted the day; I feel my empty stomach rumble. My body is not satisfied with the black coffee I had for breakfast, so I decide that the beauty salon next door will be my last search before I move onto the flats above the shops, and hopefully, find some food whilst I'm at it. I will try not to overthink it; if there are dead people up there, they can't hurt me.

Moving carefully into the salon through its giant window (now devoid of glass, which crunches under my feet), I almost have to shade my eyes from the garish pink walls. It's a small shop, with a big mirror along one wall, designed to make it look bigger, and it's cracked in places, but I catch a glimpse of myself and frown. I'm paler than I ever remember being, and that's saying something for a redhead. I've lost weight, and I look homeless. Torn and muddy clothes, dirty skin, knotted hair. I'm pretty sure I smell like I'm homeless, too. Maybe I will wash tonight. Undeterred, I continue through the salon and take a glance into their small bathroom in the back. *Jackpot!*

Sitting on a shelf above the toilet is a pack of tampons. Undisturbed, like they were waiting to be found. I rush to count them: six left. There's also a pack of aspirin.

'Missed that one, didn't you!' I direct smugly to absolutely no one. I stuff my finds into my backpack and prepare to leave. Absolutely delighted. I step back into the street and an icy breeze hits my face. The weather is changing: I notice dark clouds speeding above my head, and I'm not far from Maggie's. I know she can have a hot stew cooking in next to no time, so I contemplate if there's time before it gets dark, but something is off.

It takes me a second to realise there's a fast-growing vibration, which causes slithers like cold water down my spine, followed by the familiar screaming roar. Motorbikes! The sounds hammer into my chest, rousing me into action as the whines come quickly, amplified by the empty streets, and I panic. I need to hide.

Sprinting from the salon, I trip over my own feet and land on my knees and my left hand, glass ripping through my skin. It stings, and I feel blood trickle from the cuts, but I can't stop. I push myself back up as the screeching of tyres comes closer. I'm so angry with myself. *Why didn't I hear them sooner? Why wasn't I paying more attention to my surroundings?*

'Shit!' I exclaim to myself as I race down an alleyway opposite the salon. A black cat jumps down from a bin and runs away, just as the bikes enter the high street. I press close to the wall and crouch low. The deafening machines hurtle by one at a time and I put my hands to my ears as they pass. They don't slow, or stop, and after a few minutes, the noise has subsided to a distant whir. I'm shaken. These unwelcome visitors are becoming more frequent, and they're dangerous. I eventually stand from my spot and assess my wounds. Not as bad as I thought, but my hand is throbbing as I pull out a shard of glass. I improvise, taking out my hair bobble, letting my red locks fall in front of my eyes and mouth, causing me to swear as I fluster around in my bag for one of the tampons. I unravel it into a suitable size and create a makeshift bandage.

'Florence bloody Nightingale,' I whisper sarcastically. My heart is racing, and I feel sick with the adrenaline.

I decide I will go back home, not to Maggie's. Maggie will baby me, she will see my bleeding wounds and tell me how I'm not surviving well enough, how I'm not coping, but I'm too stubborn to take note of this. I just want to feel the safety of my little brick house right now.

Taking slow steps and keeping close to the buildings, or using objects to hide behind, I track back to the quarry road, back to the desolate pathways and rural countryside roads that lead me into my village.

My village.

Deadly silent, except for the rustle of trees, and the familiar, soothing songs of the birds and the insects.

My safe, empty village.

I know this because I've been into every neighbouring house and cottage, and I've seen all my neighbours after the virus—and stolen their food. I've seen the pets that died with them. I've covered each face with cloth, even the children and the babies. I've cried over each one of them. I've screamed at the horror behind the doors of each home. I know my village is empty, because I'm the only one here who didn't die, and now, here I am. After the carnage, after the death, here I am, still alive.

18 Months Earlier

The TV in the front room is blaring when I walk through the door; the curtains are drawn. I already feel a slight annoyance as I kick off my hi-tops.

'Dad, it's like twenty degrees outside,' I criticise.
Our humble little home has its living room directly to the right of the narrow entrance hallway, where I hang up my jacket and rucksack. The door is open, and it's dark in there. I know he will have been sitting in that spot all day whilst Mum hurries back and forth to fetch him coffee. Forty-five years she's been doting on him, and I don't know how she hasn't snapped by now.

'Hiya, love, how was your day?' he replies, unfazed by my tone. I shrug indifferently, shuffling into the room, and flop onto our blue velvet sofa.

'I thought you were both off to the garden centre today?'
I know they haven't been, or they would still be outside. Gardening is one of Dad's favourite hobbies. Once he starts, he doesn't stop for days. It's the only thing that gets him moving, and I feel like he should be doing *something* with his time.

'Tomorrow, love, the sale for tomato plants starts then.' He smiles, quickly adding,

'Have you seen this, though?'

I glance at the news he's watching, the same headline as yesterday about some deaths on the other side of the world. I roll my eyes.

'Don't tell me you've sat here all day, Dad, watching this? Where's Mum?'

'Kitchen, love.'

I give him a quick kiss on the forehead and decide to find Mum for my own sanity. As predicted, she's standing over a steaming pot of something wonderful-smelling, with vapour swirls rising high towards the ceiling of our modest little kitchen.

'Has he been stuck to that TV all day?' I fuss as she turns to greet me, her greasy apron flapping when she moves.

'Oh, leave him be, he's enjoying his retirement.' She laughs. I find myself internally cringing.

Both my parents are now retired. Dad celebrated with a party in our local pub last month, after forty years as an electrician. It was quite sweet, really. I got to listen to stories from people I'd never met and saw some Irish family we haven't seen for years. Mum, who is slightly older, has been pottering around for the last two years after she retired as an accountant for a local law firm in town. But I'm quite resentful that they're older, I don't exactly know why. They are good people, doting parents; however, it feels like we are a world apart when it comes to modern life. As an example, I really want a big party for my eighteenth next month, like my friend Alice had. Her parents hired out a swanky place in the city, with a garden gazebo and an awesome DJ, laser lights, and a fully stocked bar. We ended up dancing the night away until the early hours, and her dad was so drunk he passed out on a table and had to be carried home. My parents are in bed by 9pm religiously. It's embarrassing. Their technical ability goes as far as text messages, online shopping, and search engines. I'm constantly having to explain how to do this and that, three or four times over, and they're just not interested. I know I was a very longed-for baby, so I try to not be annoyed. Twenty years of trying to conceive, they had all but given up hoping for a child, and then *boom,* out of nowhere out came a red-headed, screaming banshee, which was me, and I loved the story, but I wish I'd come along earlier in their lives, so we could at least share some common ground.

'Dinner ready in five mins, love,' she declares.

This is a hint for me to get out the cutlery and set up the folding tables so we can eat in front of the TV. I've been home about ten minutes and already feel annoyed, but I make myself smile and be an obedient teenage child. Mum brings in a beautiful vegetable stew, with homemade bread rolls, dripping with butter, and places it on my little white dinner tray. She sits down, not taking off her apron, and Dad barely looks up; we pass around the salt. The news is still on, and I try to switch off, daydreaming about the party I know I'm never going to have.

'It's bad all this, isn't it, Ladybird?' Mum exclaims, pointing at the telly, and I cringe again. The 'cute' nickname has long outworn itself.

'Can we just try calling me Elle?' I sigh.

'No,' cuts in Dad. 'That's not your name.'

'Neither is Ladybird,' I retort.

We eat in relative silence, as the 24-hour news stream that Dad is obsessed with blares out scaremongering claims of a supervirus piercing through China, killing hundreds each day. I burst out laughing, much to my parents' horror, and feel like I must explain myself.

'Seriously, it's such a load of crap. There's absolutely nothing on social media about a pandemic in China, nothing trending. It's political propaganda. We've just been discussing propaganda in class, in fact; this is such a classic example.'

'Not sure I agree with that, Elizabeth,' Dad pipes up.

Oh, here we go, I think. A few weeks in front of the news and we have the makings of a debate professional.

'Enlighten me?'

'Well, firstly, China is reporting the same story, first-hand, on their *own* news channels.'

He picks up the remote and quickly flicks through the 500+ channels to find one called China Central Television.

'Spending your retirement time well, I see.'

He throws me his best *mind your manners* look, and nods to the screen.

'One hundred and forty-five people have died, just today, in a little town. Just watch. The army over there is already stopping people from leaving or entering the place. They don't mess around, that's for sure.' He chuckles.

For a moment, I pay attention. There's a lot of crying, and you can see the fear on the faces on the TV, as reporters try to push their way over confused, frustrated families to thrust a microphone against their face masks.

'Still not sure what all the fuss is about, Ebola didn't get this much coverage,' I say.

After tea, I help Mum wash up, and finally take sanctuary in my bedroom, walking into the smart steel grey and forest green colours I decorated it in last year. My bed is tidy, and my window is open, letting a nice breeze saunter into the room. I reach into the pocket of my jeans before I lie down on the bed, deciding to process some of the group chats I'm part of, and read the first of no less than seven messages from my best friend, Emma. These are mainly focused on her current boyfriend, and how he hasn't made any comments on her socials since last week. She complains in detail how another one of our friends spotted him laughing with a girl we know, in a bar in town at the weekend. *This doesn't sound like the crime of the century,* I think, but I know Emma is expecting outrage from me, so I oblige.

I spend most of my evening texting back and forth with Emma, and somehow find myself agreeing to a night at the bowling alley at the weekend, which I really don't like the thought of. Emma and I are opposites. She is a social bee. She loves to be involved in all the drama. She spends days deciding which clothes to wear, how to style her hair, or what colour nails to have; whereas, I am happy in my own company, awkward in large groups. I am content to wear my trademark jeans and dark baggy hoodies. I often think it's because of where we grew up. I grew up here. This sleepy old rural hamlet, with only a post office, a corner shop, and a quarry for company. It's a forty-minute bus ride into the city centre where our old school was, and my college is, whilst Emma grew up five minutes from these places, in a large townhouse on a sprawling inner-city estate. She's like a different species to me, but I guess that's why I've always liked her. I have no idea why she likes me, but we just work well together. We always have, and I think we always will.

For the rest of the evening, I shower, and do a little homework on my laptop for my media studies class. I *think* I want to follow a career in marketing, but I'm not completely sold on the idea yet. I'm taking A-levels in graphic design, business and media studies, but ironically, I try to avoid social media and my group chats as much as possible. I find them obvious, manipulative, and just dull; however, the little snippet of news I watched earlier has intrigued me. Of course, I won't tell Dad this, but if it's *not* propaganda, then I haven't seen anything like it before and that sends a shooting chill into my stomach. I notice the mainstream news has started reporting it, too, calling it a *'global threat'*, and *'a strain of SARS never before experienced'*.

They are show-stopping headlines, enough to make your heart rate pick up a beat or two, and I silently give credit to the person behind them. Maybe one day I can work for a newspaper as a journalist and create my own headlines like this. Words that make people just stop what they are doing. I read another catchy line:

'More deadly than MERS - Associated death at case-fatality ratio of 89%'

I don't even know what that is or what it means, but before I know it, I'm lost in a search engine rabbit hole, until I fall into an anxious sleep.

Present Day

Five hundred and sixty-two seconds.

That's how long it takes for the little red, dented camping kettle to boil. I know this because every time I boil it, which is sometimes three times a day, I count out the seconds slowly, until I reach the hundreds, like I used to do as a kid:

'One elephant, two elephants, three elephants...' and so on. It's painstakingly slow. The kettle's balanced precariously on an old metal grill, and I can't get much more than two mugs of coffee or instant soup at a time. But I'm so thankful for it. I find I'm thankful for a lot of things I never thought about before. Mainly the kettle, the log burner in my front room, and the grill I shoved inside it. I'm lucky it's here. Mum argued against spending money to install it; she always preferred the central heating. She said the radiators warmed up her bones, but Dad *loved* his log fire. We used it every winter, and to be fair, it was glorious when he had it blazing, bright orange flames flickering on the dark walls in our front room whilst it hailed outside, cosy, and snug indoors with the faint smell of smoky wood wafting through the house.

Without this black metal box right now, trying its hardest to burn for me, I'm not sure I would have survived up to now.

22

It's minus degrees, and I've woken up twice during the night to stoke the fire and get it going again as I've been so cold.

I'm even wearing a woolly hat, gloves, and scarf. I'm curled up in a sleeping bag with my duvet wrapped around me on the sofa, and I'm still cold. I'm not as good at getting the fire blazing as Dad used to be, but I'm starting to get better, understanding when I'm letting too much oxygen creep in, or not enough. It's a difficult balance, especially now the dried kiln wood that we had stored in the garden shed has gone, along with the wood I salvaged from our neighbour Eric's house. I'm relying on dead branches and twigs right now.

'Five hundred and thirty-two, five hundred and thirty-three...'

The kettle starts to whistle.

'Hey!' I moan. 'You're early! How have you managed that?'

I suspect the kettle has taken the same amount of time it normally takes when I fill it to the line; but I, however, have miscounted my seconds. I decide not to tell the kettle this information; I do not like to be wrong.

'I'm keeping my eye on you.'

I shuffle over and pick it up by the handle, ready to pour the water into my Pot Noodle. I'm excited. I haven't had a Pot

Noodle for ages! I guess my diet has changed drastically over these last few months, but I must eat what I can, and in my case, what I can find. I decide to add Chicken Pot Noodle to my list of things I'm grateful for when I start to eat, and the flavour trickles down my throat. I pour myself an instant black coffee with the remaining water, and let the steam warm my face. As I eat, I glance over to my depleted box of food by the front room door. Everything I have and use is in this room, except for the toilet bucket and the water containers that I store in the bathroom, but I live and sleep in here for the warmth, and find I don't use the kitchen anymore, even though there's plenty of room to store food. I've just gotten into the habit of placing whatever food I salvage into the plastic storage box we used to keep Mum's old paperwork in. The same paperwork I ended up burning a few weeks ago.

Sighing, I evaluate the box. I can see a few tins of spaghetti hoops, which are my favourite. There's some curry sauce, packets of plain noodles and pasta, tinned fruit, beans, tinned vegetables, and a tub of gravy. Theres also a massive tin of coconut milk that I'm not sure what to do with other than drink it, and plenty of packets of instant soup. I know I have enough to keep me going for a week or two, but I also know it's not going to last forever. However, after the close call with the motorbikes, and cutting my hand on the glass, I'm a little bit shaken. I'm not sure I dare venture outside any time soon to find further supplies, but at the same time, I know eventually I won't have a choice.

I eat quickly, contemplating it all. Survival is just so hard. I'm constantly worrying about something or other, and I stare at the cut on my hand. It's deeper than I thought, but I managed to clean the wound with some old vodka and wrapped it with a clean bandage from the first-aid kit. It hurts like hell. Probably needs stitches, and I *could* probably get them. Weird odds, but there's a local doctor at the other side of town who survived, too. Dr Aaron Green.
The issue is my pride.

Maggie knows him. I would have to tell Maggie about the cut, which means being fussed over and judged. I don't want that.

I decide to just sit it out and wait for it to heal. I'm also soaking it in cooled, boiled salt water each day to keep infection away, something my mum once taught me to do after having a bad tooth a few years ago. This seems to help.

In addition to my throbbing hand, I'm also worried I'm running low on water. My mind turns to this. There are two big containers in the bath: one is full of murky river water, and one is empty. Each container lasts me about a week if I don't use any of the water to wash my hair. It's so cold in the house, though, I can't imagine doing that. There's a variety of different-sized bottles down here, all full of water I've previously boiled and cooled, so I'm good for now, but it's such a long process to make the water sanitary, I know I need to address this again soon.

   I sigh again. Taking another sip from my coffee and wishing I had more noodles left. Cool winter light begins to stream through the gaps in the curtains as dawn arrives, and I'm already feeling lonely. Every so often, I glance up at our obsolete 52-inch TV, mounted to the wall above a white entertainment unit. Everything has a thick layer of dust on it now, but I imagine it switching itself on, a bright gameshow blaring out from the screen, audience laughter ringing out from the speakers. The light from the burner ignites my imagination as I remember funny snippets from programmes I used to watch, and I burst out laughing to myself. Visions of TV presenters walking up and down a studio, throwing prompt cards around and having an 'inside joke' with us, the viewers. My sad laugh echoes around the dark, dreary room, and my smile, with all the memories fades quickly. I'm forced to stare back into the flames, adding more twigs, and brushing away unwanted tears that track down my face.

At some point I drift back into sleep, and awake hours later with a start. I fell asleep almost bolt upright with my back leaning against the sofa, and pins and needles cruise through my left arm. The Pot Noodle container is on its side next to me, and the house is freezing. 'Shit.'

I'm going to need to find some paper or cardboard to get the fire going again, but before I have a chance to move or think, there's a resounding crack which vibrates down the chimney. It's the unmistakable sound of the backfire of an exhaust, and the familiar distant whine which accompanies it. 'Shit!'

I push away the bed covers quickly, bustle out of the sleeping bag, and sprint to the kitchen at the back of the house. The window here is easy to open. A slight press of my thumb on the latch, and cold air blasts onto my face. Palpitations start in my chest. I can hear the bikes clearer. They sound like they're on the main road. I stay still for what feels like an age, listening to the noises whirring up and down. *Why are they in my village? Why are they in MY village?*

Engines stop, start, stop again. They are moving closer to me minute by minute, and doing something with all the starting and stopping, but I can't tell what it is.
Maybe they spotted smoke from my chimney?

I shut the window and run to Dad's utility cupboard under the stairs. There's a hammer here. God knows why I think I'm brave enough to use it; I know I'm not, but I feel safer just holding it. I suddenly hear the screech of tyres enter my street, then stop. An engine ticking over.

Instantaneously, I rush through the hallway and leap up the stairs two at a time into our spare little box room. full of old shoes, clothes, boxes of family photos and such. The window here looks onto the front garden and the driveway. Immediately I can see the bikes.

One of the guys has a notebook and pencil in hand, and they are all dressed in black from head to toe, wearing balaclavas. I'm shaking like a leaf, careful not to be noticed as I peer through the blinds. The guy without the notebook is counting the cars on the street, his hand pointing at each one, including Dad's old Nissan. They seem to have a brief argument and I think I figure out what's going on. They are deciding which cars are electric, and which are diesel or petrol, and are noting it down. After a minute, they turn around and move on.

There's a sick lump in my throat. I know these people. As they ride away, I see it: the crude white symbol drawn in some kind of paint or pen on the backs of their jackets. An upside down cross.

I've seen what these people do, what they are capable of. They call themselves 'The Chosen'. I curse. They will come back. They must be venturing away from the city, or wherever they are held up, looking to loot from the smaller, untouched places like my village. I remain in the box room, clutching the hammer long after they leave the street. I am going to *have* to go and see Maggie now. At least inform her, advise her to be careful when she goes about her business, but she probably already knows. Surely, she heard the bikes herself over the last few days? and I guess I shouldn't worry too much. Maggie is a *real* survivor. I feel like I'm completely clueless in comparison, hanging on by a thread.

At fifty-two years old, I don't think she's scared of anything, or anyone. She has a plethora of knowledge about all kinds of things she tries to teach me. Like using baking powder for toothpaste, ginger for pain relief, and she always has baskets full of edible mushrooms, berries, and plants to share with me. I remember the first time I met her at the church in town. I was broken, and she was just this strong, grey-haired warrior woman who picked me up, and kept me fighting. She helped me collect the bodies of my parents after they had passed away, driving her vintage yellow-and-orange VW to my house to bring them to the mass cremation in the graveyard. Unfazed, resilient. I had even smiled to myself as I thought of Dad's reaction, that his journey to his final resting place would be in the back of a hippy van.

But then I think about The Chosen. I saw the fear in her eyes that day we encountered them for the first time, although she has never spoken about it.

Eventually, I put down my hammer. The cul-de-sac is safe for now, and I doubt they will come back today. I'm guessing they are just scouting for now. It will be a big operation, siphoning fuel. They will need containers, and a truck to carry it all in. *They must have all this,* I think. Then, I wonder just how big The Chosen are. How many of them are in this gang, that ravishes the remains of society like a pack of wild wolves?

For the remainder of the day, I'm so jumpy. The slightest noise and I'm like a meerkat. I know I'm buying time, because I don't want to admit *I need her*. I potter around the house doing some jobs I have neglected, scrubbing some underwear and socks, and hanging them to dry in the garden. It feels weirdly futile knowing danger is making plans to return, but I'm still here, pretending everything is normal.

    I pace the garden. I check on Mum's rainwater tank, which was installed for the plants and flowers. Now I keep my eye on it as a back-up water supply. A last resort in case the river dries up, or if I'm injured and can't make the walk to the bankside. Having the tank here, sloshing around, keeps me calm. I then turn my attention to the small greenhouse. Everything in there is dead. I unintentionally let the tomatoes, cucumbers, onions, and peppers die in summer. I have no idea how to grow them, but Maggie says she will come and have a look in the springtime, confident she can revive everything. In the meantime, I am to harvest what I need from the allotment in town that she painstakingly attends to each day.

    I take a moment to sit on our garden bench, staring at the long, unkempt yellow grass and the weeds that were never there before, and looking at the open manhole in the corner where I pour out my toilet bucket, I frown. Dad would be mortified; he kept this garden so perfectly green and manicured. I'm failing, I know I am failing at surviving, and it's pathetic. I'm annoyed there are tears starting to creep into my eyes, as though validating my uselessness.

But I'm only nineteen for God's sake, I was looking forward to my life so much. I was looking forward to my gap year, volunteering in the Maldives, snorkelling with turtles in Greece. It was all planned in my head what the future might look like. I was going to be a journalist, or a photographer. I even had a boyfriend; I even think we were in love.

Now it's gone.
It's all gone, just like the garden, just like my parents, just like me, if I can't get my act together. I fall to my knees and scream, ripping the weeds up with my bare hands.

'I HATE YOU!' Meaning the virus, and everything it has taken from me. 'I HATE YOU!'

I pick up a stone and launch it purposefully at the greenhouse. The lone smash isn't enough.

Another stone: it shatters more, then another and another until glass and carnage lie across the garden and I scream in a hopeless rage, which turns into sobs. I drop to my knees completely distraught.

'I want you back!'

I cry hard. Barely realising I have fallen forward and curled into a ball, the grass enveloping me. Gasping for air as I pant every word.

'I, want… you, mum. I want…you, dad, I. *NEED. YOU. BACK! Please come back to me!*'.

It sounds childish, the words ringing in my ears, but I can't change the helplessness I feel.

On his deathbed I promised dad I would live, for him. That I would carry on, for him. We weren't to know I would actually be a *survivor*; it was just something to say to relieve the pain of saying goodbye. But here I am. Alive. When they are all dead, and it hurts so much.

Woefully, I stay like this for an age, rocking back and forth, repressed grief tearing at my soul. I whisper one last time before I close my swollen eyes. *'I want you back'*.

16 Months Earlier

With my eyes shut, I let the beat of the song pound into my veins, each thud, each thunderous roll of the baseline in tune with my body. Smoke from the machine stings my throat, and lasers blind my vision, but I love the sensation, feeling the rhythm and the tempo like I am part of the music as I sway my arms and hips in a trancelike motion. I'm not even sure I know this tune, but I don't care anymore. The cocktails have made me lightheaded and carefree.

It may only be a nightclub in the city, and not the party I had wanted, but this, I think, is *my* night. I open my eyes to look for Emma. The sea of sweating, gyrating bodies all around hides her for a moment, but I'm positioned on a raised platform, overlooking the heads of the mass of people below, and then there she is. Busy in the corner with an unknown man, her mouth clamped on his as she thrusts her red dress against him and moves to the music. It's almost like she can feel me looking at her, and she opens one eye to catch my gaze. I smile and give a thumbs-up. I'm happy for her. Actually, I'm over the moon. She's been through hell with her ex these last few weeks, and I'm proud she finally got the strength to move on from him, the using bastard, he was. I leave her to it and turn to jump down, leaving my spot, which is instantly filled by two others as I navigate my way to the bar. I'm wearing a navy-blue skirt with a nice lacy white top Emma bought me, and some kitten-heeled shoes.

I feel attractive, I guess. My hair is in beautiful waves and not tied up, although I'm way out of my comfort zone. I'm quite relieved when I get to the bar. Deep mahogany wood stretches the length of the room, stained with knocked-over drinks, and littered with discarded straws and miniature umbrellas. I find people's attention is firmly on the bar staff as they attempt to get noticed, and I'm happy to just wait. It's 1am already, but Emma's dad has arranged to pick us up at 2am, so I know there is plenty of time for another drink. I spend a ridiculous amount of time looking at the cocktails list chalked on a blackboard, trying to decide which one to go for, and laugh at the rude names. I'm practically lost in a daydream when a voice speaks directly to me over the throbbing melody.

'It's Elizabeth, isn't it?'

I look up into dark, handsome eyes, behind curls that fall in front of them, trying to place the face.

'Elle,' I correct, and smile. 'Sorry, do we know each other?'

'Ouch.'

He feigns hurt, clasping his hand over his heart, when I see a tribal tattoo on his knuckles, etched into his bronze skin. He's so hot.

'You don't recognise me, I'm wounded.'

I smile shyly, taking a guess: 'College?'

He grins, waiting for me to expand my knowledge. Then my brain suddenly clicks into gear, and I feel so embarrassed.

'Oh, God yes! Sorry, you're in the mechanic's class... my friend's brother's' friend.'

He cracks up laughing, a mischievous twinkle in his eye.

'That's all I am to you, your friend's brother's' friend?'

I avert my eyes bashfully. How did I not recognise him? We must have passed like ships in the wind for ten years. Emma's brother Edward, almost two years older, always had his mates hanging around, but I never paid any of them much attention, if I'm being honest. Emma and Edward didn't get along as kids, always fighting, Emma never afraid to give him a bust lip, but I guess things change when you grow up. They are quite close these days.

'Sorry. I don't know your name.'

He grins and pretends he's cleaning a glass, to buy some more time.

'Danny. Can I get you a drink?'

I make a ridiculous stuttering sound and change my cocktail choice instantly from the cringeworthy sexual name of the drink I wanted, to a less embarrassing one that I don't know the taste of.

'Cosmopolitan, please.'

'You have any ID?' he asks quite seriously.

Shit, I must look like a deer in headlights. I'm still a week off my actual birthday, and I momentarily panic. I haven't been asked for ID all night. I stare at him open-mouthed for a minute, but there's that twinkle in his eye again, and without waiting for my response, he turns to make the drink. I realise I have been holding my breath and take the opportunity to release it, my heart fluttering wildly. At this moment, I feel hands squeeze my shoulders.

'Hey, what are you getting?'

Emma's timing couldn't be more off.

'Oh hi, Em, managed to pull yourself away?'

She laughs, unabashed. 'He tasted of liquorice vape, grossed me out.'

'You didn't look grossed out!' I holler, and we both burst out laughing.

Two black plastic bar stools have become available. Emma drags them over and we sit chatting and laughing, until Danny returns with a triangular-shaped glass that oozes with deep red liquid, a lime delicately placed on the side, the classic umbrella stuck into it soon to be discarded with the others. He hands the glass to me, and I swear his finger lingers on mine a second longer than required, as he glances politely at Emma.

'Ah, the friend whose brother I am acquainted with.'

'Dan the man!' She squeals and stretches over the bar to give him a dramatic kiss on the cheek, her red dress barely covering her arse as she bends.

'Ed never said you were working here now!'

'I'm a man of many secrets,' he says with a grin, replying to Emma, but looking at me. Emma notices the small gesture.

'Have you two met before? You must have surely seen each other 'round at our house over the years.'

Danny nods. 'We were just discussing this. Elle used to have a massive crush on me! She's just told me now.'
I nearly spit out the sip of alcohol I in my mouth.

'Oh my God!' I laugh, whilst shaking my head at Emma. She grins knowingly.

'Watch this one, Elle, he's too smooth.'

38

Danny holds up the card machine, staring at me whilst I fumble awkwardly with my handbag, trying to pay. Emma, who is now distracted by the new tune that's playing, shuts her eyes, swaying on the chair. Danny leans his head close to mine, and whispers in my ear, loud enough for me to hear him over the music.

'I may have had a crush on you, though.'
I think I must look stupid, as I go mute and giggly. He gives me a wink, before he's called to serve another customer.

For the last hour, I am driven to distraction with thoughts of Danny on my mind. We dance and flirt a little more, and eventually decide to leave the club, to find gravy-covered chips, and Emma's dad. The cruel feel of the sobering night air makes me realise I've drunk way too much, but my ears are ringing and my senses buzzing after hours and hours of dancing. I am happy.

'You had a good night, Elle?' Emma asks, smiling.
She knows it takes a lot for me to allow myself to loosen up, and she really wanted me to enjoy celebrating my 18th. She's the best friend I could wish for.

'I love you, Em,' I slur, linking my arm in hers. 'I had a great night. Thank you.'
She smiles warmly. 'Me too.'

We spot Emma's dad, parked in his white BMW where he said he would be. She climbs in the front, kissing his cheek, and I hop into the back, the cold leather seats on my bare legs.

'Hi, Daddy.'

'Hey, Mr M,' I say.

He smiles, not fazed by being out so late.

'Evening, ladies, I trust you had a good night?'

'Fantastic, Dad,' Emma gushes. 'Thanks for collecting us.'

We pull away from the street, and I see so many drunk people through the window. Women crying, men fighting, bouncers trying to gain control, people on the floor, people vomiting on the pavement. It's like a different world. I'm suddenly thankful I don't live in the city.

'It might be the last night out you get in a while,' Emma's dad says abruptly as we join the main road and trundle slowly towards their estate.

'Why?' Emma asks indignantly, and I look at his concerned, distressed eyes through the rear-view mirror.

'The government, they're calling for a lockdown,' he answers. 'Me and your mum have been watching the news all night. It was announced earlier; you'd already left for the night, but they're talking about closing all the schools, and the restaurants, all the bars and cinemas and anywhere people congregate. Even churches.'

'Don't be ridiculous!' Emma gasps.

I wait to see if it's a joke, but his eyes don't flicker. Instead, he turns on the car radio for us to hear for ourselves. There's an argument going on. Two voices debating if a lockdown will be legal, and ethical. If the government has a right to close businesses that rely on footfall through the door. How long might a lockdown last for?

I'm much too drunk to really absorb much of the information, but sober enough to know this is sounding pretty bad.

'Will this mean college is going to shut?' I mumble.

'But no one's sick, Dad! The sickness is abroad, it's not here!' Emma protests.

'Well, apparently, it is here,' he replies, and with those words, I feel my blood run cold.

'They're saying three people have died in London already, but it's under control. The lockdown is a precaution.'

I sit forward, confused.

'Then why not lock down London?'

Emma's dad nods to me. 'That's what we said.'

I sit back again. We're almost at their house and I can feel tiredness grip my body. I don't have any energy to worry, or to understand the weight of what's been happening in the real world whilst I have been living in my beautiful bubble of music, movement, and alcohol. But the news has caused the bubble to pop somewhat, and I'm agitated as the car stops and we stumble into the house.

The rest of the weekend flies by in a whirl of hangover and plain dumbstruck disbelief at what is happening. When I finally crawl home, I go straight back to bed and lie there watching news reports, reading comments and feeds, and watching videos of influencers either outraged or supportive of a country-wide lockdown. I watch CNN. They discuss the number of deaths across the world, desperate countries that have been in a virus hellhole for weeks already, crying out for help and medicine. Mass graves, children screaming, families weeping, and lockdowns ordered in every major capital around the world. There are thousands of dead, and it's frightening viewing.

I don't leave the comfort of my duvet, except to get paracetamol, water, and toast. Mum tries to keep my spirits up, after learning that the lockdown starts the day before my eighteenth, but I'm sulking hard. All plans are cancelled, and via a text message, the college informs me that all belongings must be collected before next Friday, when the lockdown begins. We can only attend college next week to hand in coursework and pick up our stuff, so I plan to go on Tuesday. It all feels too surreal. Like I can't comprehend how things can just shut down, but I get it. We must protect our country from this virus that just seemed to appear from nowhere, and no one can understand or agree on where it started, why it started, or how to stop it.

Doctors are baffled, autopsies offer confusing information, and trial vaccines are being pushed through in America and Europe. Of course, there are already people protesting this, and some are using violence to be heard.

At some point I sigh heavily, feeling completely helpless. I switch my phone off, pull the duvet over my head again, and bury my frustrations and anxieties in the soft, warm fabric. I sleep, and mope like a spoiled, miserable child until Tuesday morning. This was not how I envisioned my eighteenth birthday to be.

The bus is surprisingly quiet. It comes to a halt with a hiss before me and as I embark, I notice some people have purchased blue medical masks. They look ridiculous. The bus driver smirks at me, as though he knows what I am thinking; he is not wearing a mask. I take my seat and watch the world from the window.

Other than these masks, nothing else looks too different as we trundle toward the city. The bus stop is directly outside college. It's a modern building on the corner of an intersection. Big silver panels, and long glass windows trimmed with blue lights, loom over the street. There's usually a throng of students at this time, hanging around the front of the building. Vaping, chatting, shuffling between classes. Today, there is a mere handful, heads down, some with masks on; anxious, bewildered faces on everyone I see. I walk the near empty corridors, heading to my class. I'm not sure what to expect. Will my classroom even be open?

My question is answered when I reach the door to find the lights off and the door locked.

'Great,' I hiss.

How am I supposed to get my coursework now? I pace around for a few minutes, hoping someone turns up, and I check my phone to see if I've had any replies on my chat group. I have. I open the message to read that all our coursework has been brought into the canteen, and we must find the table labelled with our classroom details. My trainers echo on the shiny floor as I wind towards the hall, and my footsteps are soon joined by a quiet bustle of people shuffling around white plastic tables placed in uniform rows. The canteen has been transformed into a sombre collection point for all the students, and I see hand-written scrawled posters sellotaped to each table with the course name on. There's a messy array of boxes, files, folders, and books covering the ground, with beautiful half-painted drawings, and sculptures displayed around what I imagine is the art and design area.

'Elizabeth, known as Elle!'

The smooth voice trickles over the room, the acoustics making the words louder than they need to be. I whip my head around and already feel myself blushing. Danny is walking over to me, an infectious smile on his face.

'Oh, if it isn't my friend's brother's friend,' I quip, which has the desired effect of making him laugh. I smile outwardly, but inside, my stomach is in knots. I feel frumpy in my black hoodie and jeans, and clumsy as I try walking steadily to where I know my coursework sits.

'Did you have a good weekend?' he asks, walking with me.

'Yes, thank you. Actually. It was a great night. Did you?' I ask, internally cringing. Why would he have had a good night? He was working. What a stupid question.

'I met a hot redhead,' he answers instantly, grinning, awaiting my response.

I throw him a bashful glance, unsure what to say to his heavy flirting. Emma has tried to warn me, he's a bit of a player. I decide to change tack.

'Have you got what you need today? Your coursework?' He takes the hint, and I see a playful smirk.

'There are a few books I need to pick up, but yeah. Most of the work we do is manual. I just want my books; they were expensive, and I'll be damned if I'm leaving them here to go missing while this all blows over.'

'You think it will blow over?'

We reach my table together, where I start thumbing through the folders to find my paperwork. He shakes his head.

'I hope so, but it's all a bit mental, to be honest, isn't it?'

I nod. 'What's your plans, whilst this place is shut down?' I see that cheeky smile start at his lips and continue up into his eyes.

'Is that an invitation?'

The unfavourable trait of being a redhead strikes again as colour creeps up my neck and face.

'Maybe,' I answer cautiously.

'Maybe?' he repeats.

I feel electric energy bouncing between us as he takes a step closer to me, forcing me to turn to face him. His shoulders sit a foot higher than my own, and he bends down towards me, where I can feel his hot, anticipating breath in my ear. He's ridiculously confident.

'How about I get your number, and we make our own entertainment?'

A loud cough from one of the college professors breaks the tension, and Danny steps away, holding my gaze. I exhale a small breath and smile, trying to compose myself. Looking into his expectant eyes, I say, 'You can have my number'.

Present

I switch my torch on. It's been a disturbed, sleepless night in my bleak front room. I point it at the ceiling, I have tried to sleep, but it's too cold and I'm on edge. I switch it off.

   I have completely run out of wood, so I point it at the empty wicker basket next to the log burner in case something has appeared inside. I switch it on again. There still isn't anything there.

   I switch it off.
Yesterday, I hadn't left myself any time for foraging before dark. I was too frightened to venture off my estate and spent a ridiculous amount of time moving the fridge from the kitchen and outside into the garden. With the strength of an ox, I dragged that asshole all the way, propping it up against the garden gate with grunts, groans, and almost a burst blood vessel. At the time it made me feel safe, now I'm just annoyed with myself for wasting time and energy. My stomach gripes loudly, distracting my thoughts, and I switch my torch on again. I direct the thin stream of light at the box of porridge oats. Then I click it off.

   I've been contemplating eating them with cold water, but the porridge is over there, and I'm here on the sofa under my blankets. All my bowls are unwashed *again*. I point my light at the stack of pots on the side. They haven't moved.

I switch it off.

Maybe I could reuse one of the bowls, maybe the one that I used for porridge the other day? I lie thinking about the porridge for another twenty minutes.

I see the blue-grey hues of morning light through the gap in the curtains and decide to wait until daylight, for that crust of warmth the winter sun might give through the window. My eyes feel sore from lack of sleep, my head fuzzy. My hair is unbrushed, my teeth unclean, and I'm desperate for the toilet, but I know the bucket is full.

I hate the bucket.

I hate having to squat over it, and hate having to walk to the bottom of the garden to empty the contents.

When I have no more excuses left, I make myself leave the sofa. I stand, letting the sleeping bag fall to the carpet, and the instant chill sweeps over my body. I tug open the curtains, and glance at the frozen world outside the window. There's a fox on the street; I've seen it before. It weaves in and out of all the gardens, hunting for scraps. It doesn't stick around long, but it makes me think; *how does it know how to survive?* I turn back to the room and take the crusty bowl from the stack, trying not to look at it, or overthink. I can't wash it properly—there's no liquid or soap left—so I add the new porridge and half a bottle of water, then search for the small tub of cinnamon to sprinkle over the sloppy, cold oats. It tastes as expected, like small pieces of wet cardboard drowned in sweet spice. I eat it all.

I wonder what time it is. I have no concept of time anymore. Everything I ever had needed charging to make it work, and Dad went to the pyre with the only battery-powered watch in the house.

I have thought several times about finding a watch in one of the neighbouring homes, but I can't. Even when I must scavenge for food, I feel like I'm stealing. It's stupid, it's pathetic, and it's probably going to kill me, but I can't bring myself to take their things. So, I guess the time. Maybe 7am, maybe 8am. Maggie should be awake by now, and it will take me an hour to walk via the quarry, the safest way, so I decide to set off as soon as I'm ready.

Maggie still lives in the house she had shared with her husband of thirty years. A brick terrace townhouse, one amongst many in a warren of winding streets near the primary school and community gardens where she grows her vegetables. Like me, she is the only survivor on her street. Unlike me, she actively goes out of her way to find and meet with other survivors. She networks with people, trades items and swaps gossip, usually arranging to meet at her allotments, where she can offer fresh food in exchange for anything she needs. I think this is risky, and one day she will get hurt. Survivors are desperate people.

There's a thick mist this morning as I climb over the quarry gates and land with both feet on the other side. The birds are not as chirpy, and it feels cold, ominous. I can't see far in front of me, and I don't like it. I've brought the hammer, the only weapon I have against the traumatised, angry leftovers of humanity I might encounter, and I grip the rubber handle hard. I listen carefully as I walk onwards, only the laughing cry of a woodpecker startling me.

Climbing through the fences and weaving my way up the meadows and onto the silent tarmac streets of the town, my senses are heightened, but there's no whine of engines today. Even so, my hands are clammy. Mist seems to linger thicker here, distorting the red-brick houses that sit as permanent, silent crypts, as I jump over potholes and cracks in the road where weeds and brambles have flourished. I navigate my way around the eerily still vehicles, some parked, some abandoned with others that had been destroyed in the riots, and I amble up the hill towards Maggie's street, just as freezing rain starts to fall.

Three slow but loud knocks and wait. That's the code. The rain is falling heavier now, and I pull my hoodie over my head, tucking in the red strands of hair that are fast becoming drenched. I know Maggie has installed about fifty locks and bolts since the rioting days, and I know she has a shotgun, and is probably very able to use it without a second thought. She won't open the door until she knows it's safe, watching from behind the shroud of her net curtains in the upstairs window. I shuffle on the spot to keep warm, staring at the crumbling brick wall in her front yard. There's a rustle before the door opens, then a moment of quiet nerves. She will be the first person I've spoken to in over a month.

'Come in, child! Ack, you're frozen to the bone!' Maggie's heavy Scottish accent makes me smile as she embraces me warmly, tightly. Even though I'm dripping wet, she squeezes me for longer than is required and I realise I have a lump in my throat, and my eyes are wet, not only with the rain. When we break free, I see she has tears, too. Her hand bats them away and she smiles, as if she is foolish.

'Come in, Elle. Oh, it's been too long. I have been so worried about you.'

I step around her, passing her in the tiny hallway as she re-locks the door and I continue toward the back of the house where the kitchen feels warm, emitting a glorious smell. The garden backs onto another house, encasing her safely, so Maggie spends most of her time in this room, where roamers, scavengers, or gangs like The Chosen can't see her pottering around. I discard my backpack and wait for her to join me. *She looks thinner,* I think, as she shuffles towards me with a big grin, her hair grey and straw-like, and there's wrinkles when she smiles, which I'd not noticed before.

'Have you eaten lately? You look half-starved,' she clucks at me, pointing me to a seat at a small dining table that has a bundle of knitting there. I move the wool to one side gently, deciding not to mention that I also think she looks half-starved, too!

'New jumper?' I ask, commenting on her knitting.

'Blanket, actually. It's so cold at night, I'm trying to get it done before the temperature drops any further.'

'You're so talented, Maggie, will you show me how?'

She nods enthusiastically. 'Of course, of course. You can knit hats and gloves once I show you and come with me to trade them.'

I frown. She tries so hard to get me to interact with her new idea of trading things and meeting people. She is fully aware of how I feel, but I let it go, and glance around the room instead, my eyes falling greedily on a large and complex stove with orange pipes connected to a gas cylinder.

'Whoa, Maggie!' I exclaim, jumping up and pointing. A pan of hot broth sits bubbling away nicely. She walks over to it, turns off the gas, and looks at me, beaming.

'I've had it about two weeks. I traded it for seeds, would you believe it, and Jeff's old pedal bike. That's all they wanted. Even helped me get it home.'

My excitement suddenly drops, along with my stomach.

'They", Maggie? Who's *they*?'

Please don't tell me she has been naive enough to lead strangers to her door! I have never even shown her where I live! But as I listen, it sounds horribly like she has.

'They call themselves The Hive. A big group, from all over the place, who came together from communicating on a radio or something. There's a big farm about twenty miles east, by the river. They live there, completely self-sufficient, with gas stoves like this, and more. He says they have animals, crops, vegetables, and can come back every month. I heard them arriving in town before I saw them. A big racket with horses and carts, dogs, and even children. I knew they would be something special.'

'Maggie, you showed them where you live! They could come back anytime and take back all the things you traded, kill you and take all your stuff!'

'Poppycock,' she exclaims. 'What would be the point of that, when I am the one who can bring traders together?'

'Are you kidding, Maggie?' *Okay, breathe.* 'Did you notice any weapons? Did they have guns?'

Maggie turns to dish out the stew, not answering.

'Brilliant,' I chip sarcastically. 'So, you've openly led people with guns to your house, people who can come back at any time. Why not just put a poster in the window for The Chosen?'

'They're nothing like The Chosen,' she sighs. 'They don't murder vulnerable people.'

'How do you know?'

Again, she doesn't answer, and I feel my heartbeat elevating. What if they are staking out her place? Waiting for the right opportunity, waiting to see who may come and visit her, like me, and I suddenly feel terribly vulnerable. She passes me a steaming bowl, as if she'd been expecting me, and sits down with her own at the table.

'Thank you,' I mutter, knowing this will be my only hot meal for a few days unless I get my act together.

We eat in silence, both frustrated with the other, which is hard because the food is so good. After a while, Maggie sighs again, and looks me in the eye, her hazel eyes softening.

'I can't live like you, Elle, alone. I can't survive like that. I need people.'

Her words sting: does she think I am enjoying surviving on my own? I am not, but we both know the depravity of society. We have both lived through the riots, been chased through the streets, and been threatened to be murdered over the slightest potential that we might have been carrying food. We had both watched the TV before the electricity stopped and saw how desperate people tore at each other over a bag of flour. Fighting with the army, burning down the shops, storming the cities and the government, public executions in the street. It was biblical; it was traumatising. Then the gangs came, like The Chosen, who even now prowl the streets to take what they want of everything left behind. No hesitation in killing anything that stands in their way.

I know she means well. She has great fantasies of a communal future, like the hippy I think she once was. Where everyone grows food in the sunshine, and there is laughter and joy, not fear and exhaustion.

I am thoughtful when I reply.

'You need people you can trust, Maggie. You can't trust these people. You're in danger now, just being here. You're always telling me to come and live with you, why don't you come and live with me? They won't know where you've gone. We could even take a car if there's any in town still with fuel, and squeeze the new stove in, and your things, and drive to mine. It's not far, and it's safe where I am.'

She smiles at me like I am a child with no idea about how the real world is.

'I'm not in any danger, Elle.'

The conversation has exasperated me. I sigh, and change the subject, not that it's any lighter a topic of conversation.

'I actually came here to warn you about The Chosen; I've seen them around over the last few days.'

'I already know,' she murmurs. She stands to take the bowls to her little washing-up bucket, and lights a candle, bringing it over to the table for warmth.

'I went to see Tim Fletcher a few days ago.'

I groan internally. I don't like or trust Tim Fletcher, an odd man who talks to himself. He has taken over the biscuit factory on one of the industrial estates. He lives within the gated complex with five Alsatians and a couple of guns he acquired in the riots. I'm pretty sure he feeds dead people to his dogs. Maggie likes to bring him fresh vegetables and tea bags every now and then in exchange for gossip. He has a trading network of his own set-up, which includes The Chosen, and I hate that she risks going there, but I decide not to comment on my dislike of Tim Fletcher. Maggie has had enough of my opinion for one day, so instead, I ask her what he has said.

'He says they are hunting for fuel for their vehicles.'
I nod; that confirms my suspicions. But then Maggie chews her lip, like she is nervous to say the rest to me.

'I will be honest with you Elle, he also said that a few weeks ago, a handful of them came to him to trade goods, and they had two women with them. Badly beaten, ropes around their necks like animals.'

I blink. 'Shit. Like slaves?'

Maggie shrugs. 'I think so.'

'Didn't Tim do anything?'

'Of course he didn't. He's a lot wiser than you think, Elle. They would have killed him.'

I feel myself shudder, processing the information. That is the worst kind of news. I really don't want Maggie to go to see Tim again, or even wander around town on her own, but what can I do?

Each not wanting to upset the other with our difference of opinion, we spend the rest of the day chatting about almost everything else other than The Chosen and The Hive, even though there is now a heavy feeling in my gut.

We have grown close over this last year, and I think we both realise we must love each other by now, and that we have replaced all the people we have lost and loved, with each other. However, we are both strong-willed and stubborn. Me more so than Maggie, which I have realised because of my refusal to run to her when I need her. From my point of view, I might be pretty useless in this apocalypse, but I've made a promise to myself that I will learn how to do everything on my own, even if it kills me.

When I decide to leave, she hands me a bag of supplies like always, and asks for nothing in return. I know there will be fresh food, herbs, and useful bits and pieces in the bag. I smile and hug her tightly before whispering, 'Just watch your back with these Hive people, Maggie, please, for my sake if not yours.'

She gives a quick nod. 'When will I see you again, Elle? Please don't leave it too long this time'.

I think for a moment. 'In a week, if the streets are safe. I'll bring you some tradeable stuff, to say thank you for these.'

'You know you don't need to, Elle. I worry about you out there all alone.'

I suppress a smirk at the irony.

'Okay, until next week,' she says, then closes the door behind me where I hear the locks clicking back into place.

For the next week, it pours. Unstoppable, relentless, freezing rain, drumming across the streets, blocking the drains, forcing all life to stay hidden and warm.

Except me.

The weather gives me no chance to replace the wood I ran out of last week. In a desperate attempt to keep warm, I end up burning anything I can find, but it's a mistake. I break up a kitchen chair, but the fumes from the white paint almost choke me. I brave the downpour and search my village for coal, logs, broken pallets, anything I can grab hold of, but end up sitting in a freezing, damp house, shivering cold by the end of the week. Completely miserable, only eating cold oats, beans. and cold, tinned stews all week, with a couple of candles to warm the room.

I almost admitted defeat yesterday—Sunday—and toyed with the idea of going to Maggie's. A day earlier than planned, but I didn't, due to whatever pride is stopping me. She's expecting me today, though, and I am out of the house as soon as the light comes. Still, it pours, but the idea of a warm drink and a fire excites me so much, I barely feel the drops bouncing off my dad's old walking jacket and down my neck. I've decided to walk direct today, following the main roads. I figure The Chosen, The Hive, and whoever the hell else is out there will not be out in this tsunami, plus I want to go to the allotment first, which is easiest to reach via this route. I want to pick some carrots or parsnips for Maggie as it will save her a trip in this weather, and I have vivid fantasies of hot soup cooking on the stove.

As I dance between walls, alleyways, and behind the cover of abandoned vehicles, my eyes dart every which way, and I listen like a rabbit. I see and hear no one. Pulling the hood of my coat tightly over my head as the rain gets heavier, I gain confidence the closer I get to the large vegetable patch, which sits behind the rows of empty streets. It has been designed in a perfect eight-hundred-metre-square plot of land, with a high metal fence and big gates, to which Maggie holds a key. The allotment houses enough growing space to satisfy around thirty to forty residents, with everything from potatoes to tomatoes, pumpkins to pomegranates. She showed me a secret entrance months ago, where part of the fence has rusted and broken away, and which is concealed by thick bushes. I have used this to enter every time, but today, as I arrive before the gates, I see they are slightly open. The lock is missing, and the chain is lying on the floor in a giant puddle. Instinctively, I look around. Other than the non-stop rain, drumming on the hard ground and on the roofs of the surrounding houses in constant, rhythmic beats, there is no other movement or noise. I step across the pool of water and push the gate further which creaks loudly.

'Maggie?'

I peer over the little sheds, and the bamboo tunnels across the expanse of land, and I'm startled to hear a dog bark back in response to my shouts, followed by a muffled cry. It's a cry I've not heard for a long time. It's the cry of a baby.

I stand, unsure what to do next, letting water drip over my face as I pull down my hood to get a wider view.

'HELLO?' I shout, hovering by the gate, ready to run. My heart hammers in my chest as the dog still barks and the baby still cries.

'Shit,' I say to myself, throwing my backpack down quickly. I unzip it and let my hammer fall into the mud. Grabbing it swiftly, I zip up the bag and stand again, half expecting someone to come running at me.

'Who's there?' I call, wielding the hammer as I step into the silent gardens before me.

I wipe rainwater from my eyes with my elbow and take a few steps closer to the sounds. I think I can see something, right at the bottom of the allotment, hidden by the tall weeds and vines wrapped around triangular canes. There's a faint wisp of smoke, too.

'Hello!' I try again, but I know my voice is quieter than last time; I can feel the tremors in my tone.

Still no reply.

I must stand for a good ten minutes: I'm drenched. My red hair has grown dark and sticks to my face, and the cry from the baby has become frantic. No other voices, though, no soothing calls, no movement. I take more steps forward, looking back over my shoulder, walking around the vegetable patches in an irregular path, trying to get a better angle. The dog is whining, I can see it from here. A dusty brown spaniel, as wet as a mop. Miserably tied up by a lead to a metal hook that sticks out from a shed. I see a pushchair, too. Thankfully, there's a rain cover over the child, but it's steamed up from inside. Every so often I see a little hand or foot press against it in an angry rage.

'Where's your mummy?' I whisper to myself, my eyes darting around, but there is literally no one else.

A steel bin, with holes perforated into the lid, holds the remaining dregs of a dying fire, and I pick up my pace towards the dog and the baby, and then I see it. A body. Lying face down in the muddy puddles.

'Shit!'

This must be the mother. It's obvious she is dead. Drops fall from the sky, splashing over her grey face. Something inside switches in me. I am no longer afraid. I sprint over the soil, almost losing my footing and falling to the uneven ground. The dog wags its tail when it sees me.

'Good boy,' I say, whilst I catch my breath.

I bend down to the body, double-checking she is dead. Her eyes are open, vacant, and surrounding her is a pool of diluted blood which has escaped from a makeshift bandage around her thigh.

'Christ.'

There's nothing I can do for her now. I turn to attend to the dog and child. Patting the dog, I soothe him. 'It's okay, boy.'

RUTH MASTERS SCIENCE FICTION AUTHOR

"Ruth's characters scream with shades of Douglas Adams and similar veins of comedic science fiction. Her imagination pops from page to page."

- Sci-Fi Now Magazine

THE LOOP
RUTH MASTERS

MOBIUS VOL.1
BELISHA BEACON & TABITHA TURNER
RUTH MASTERS

TRUXXE VOL.3
WHEN ALIENS PLAY TRUMPS
RUTH MASTERS

TRUXXE VOL.2
DO ALIENS READ SCI-FI?
RUTH MASTERS

TRUXXE VOL.1
ALL ALIENS LIKE BURGERS
RUTH MASTERS

ZEALCON VOL.2
ULTIMATE AUTOGRAPH HUNTERS
RUTH MASTERS

ZEALCON VOL.1
EXTREME AUTOGRAPH HUNTERS
RUTH MASTERS

RUTH MASTERS SCIENCE FICTION AUTHOR

The Truxxe Trilogy
Join Tom Bowler as he starts his job at an intergalactic service station, meeting a host of colourful aliens – some friendly, some not. From flipping burgers to saving planet Earth, the Truxxe Trilogy is as fast-moving as it is entertaining.

Zealcon
A pair of "paraquels" – two novels, telling the same story from the perspectives of different characters who are all on the same mission… to travel through time collecting autographs from the great and good of history.

Belisha Beacon & Tabitha Turner
Two women, four hundred years apart, wake up in each other's bodies and each other's lives in this thought-provoking novel.

The Loop
Dark and dystopian, this newly published novella follows a cast of 24th century humans and their escape from pollution and population control into a new paradise.

ruthmastersscifi.com

He seems incredibly friendly. I dread to think how long they've been out in this rain, must be a few hours at least. The dog responds by shaking his body at me, trying to dry his heavy, wet coat. I stand slowly to pull the rain cover off the pushchair, glancing always at the dog, but its general disposition is unchanging.

A startled, cold toddler looks up at me, blinking away the rain drops that land in her eyes as I move the cover. I assume she's a girl, based on the pink winter jumpsuit she is encased in. She has mid-length black locks and olive skin like her mother's; she is a beautiful little thing, cheeks rosy from the air—and from screaming, no doubt.

'Hello,' I say as cheerfully as I can muster. 'I'm Elle.' She must be around two years old, maybe younger.

'I'm going to take you home, sweetie; home with me.' She looks around at the outside world, grabbing gulps of air, looking at me with confused suspicion. Then she spots her mum on the floor and fights to get out of the straps, starting to cry again with her little arms outstretched, the word 'Mama' breaking through the garbled noises.

'Shit,' I curse again, feeling a lump in my throat.

'You gotta say goodbye to Mama, sweetie. She's sleeping. Mama is tired.'

I need to get her out of this situation, and I decide I'm going to bring her to Maggie's, along with the dog. Maggie will know what to do.

15 Months Earlier

I feel my heart rate increase the closer I get, and it's not because I'm particularly over-exerting myself, it's because I've reached the railway bridge at the quarry, and I know that means I'm halfway to Danny.

The August sun is in full splendour; it's another hot day and I have brought us a bottle of lager each, packed under the picnic blanket in my rucksack. It all feels very undercover, extremely thrilling to be sneaking about under the pretence of exercising. Well, I guess we are exercising in a sense. I giggle to myself.

I take a breather at the bridge, smiling into the sun and looking down at the tracks as the light hits the metal and glistens. I am safe here.

Safe from nosy neighbours, wondering what you are doing outside of your house. Safe from catching the virus from anyone else as they are all locked away in their homes.

Everything has stopped.
No schools, colleges, restaurants, theatres. The bowling alley and cinema shut down last week. Buses and trains have stopped running, and they've even closed the airports.

The news coming out of Europe and the rest of the world is horrific. Riots have started, thousands are dying each day, despite the lockdown. The reports say that a supervirus has taken over and is spreading from house to house on the breeze. There's no food. No help. It makes me shudder; it makes me feel sick, but it's not here. Thank God it's not here.

We are a small island; we are safe.

I hear the security van before I see it, and sprint across to the hole in the fence, the glass bottles clinking in my bag as I go. I just make through before it comes around the corner, heart racing from the thrill, and I continue onwards towards town beaming with excitement as I tread over the fields. I see Danny, waiting for me as arranged at the top of the meadow, and my heart races again, but for a different reason.

Almost every day since I gave him my number, we have text, spoken and met up in secret. I smile at the thoughts. I may be eighteen now, but in my dad's eyes I'm still around twelve. I would not dare tell him I have a boyfriend, let alone that we are meeting up. He would be livid. Plus, to add to this, he is taking lockdown very seriously and reprimands me even if I am more than a few minutes late from my daily 'jogs', giving Danny and I limited time together.

'Hey, Knucklehead,' I call over, when I realise he's not seen me approaching.

He's leaning against his Ducati in the layby at the top of the hill next to the closed factory fence. He whips his head to me with his trademark cheeky smile, walking down to meet me.

'Hey, Elizabeth, known as Elle.'

We can be together here, in the long shabby grass, confidently out of the sight of anyone. I walk over and plant my lips on his smug smile. He responds by caressing my cheek and pulling my head even closer to his with the back of his hand, and I feel the electricity course through my body. He brings his other hand up to my waist and squeezes. I know he wants me. He has been tender and patient these past four weeks.

'Nice to see you too,' I tease.

I turn to my backpack and get out the picnic blanket and beers, knowing he watches my every move with lustful eyes. We sit for a while, looking at the view over the quarry I have just hiked through. In the distance, I can just about see the start of my village. It's odd, everything is deadly quiet. Usually, from this point, you would hear a hum from the motorway several miles away, the noise carrying. Not anymore, not since the world closed its doors. Now only freight lorries are allowed to make their trips to the supermarkets, which bizarrely remain open. Apparently, you can't catch the virus in the supermarket.

'I forgot the bottle opener!' I realise, sitting myself on the blanket, looking at the brown liquid sloshing around. Danny sits closely next to me. I feel his arm hairs touching my bare arms, sending shivers across my body that he is unaware of.

'Here, let me.'

He takes the bottle from my hand and puts the lid to his mouth, struggling trying to pop it open with his teeth. I laugh.

'You're going to chip a tooth!'

He shakes his head, and a second later I hear the hiss of release as he passes it back.

'Show off,' I joke.

He does the same to his bottle and we clink them in a little cheer to ourselves. I feel incredibly nervous, but I am internally smiling at the thought of phoning Emma tonight and giving her the gossip. I obviously mentioned my plans to her yesterday, so she is waiting with repressed excitement for the news that her best friend is no longer a virgin.

'How's your family?' I ask him, attempting to douse the flames I feel inside. I know he lives at home with his mum and two younger sisters, on the same street as his aunties and cousins. They are all very close. He talks about his sisters a lot. The way he cares for them and loves them is heartwarming.

'They are fine. The twins are driving me insane, though, making stupid videos and doing ridiculous challenges.'

'Oh?' I laugh.

Danny's twin sisters are fourteen, and I've seen this craze on social media where people post videos of themselves doing all sorts of stupid stuff.

'They made me do a dance with them last night and are now threatening to upload it.'

I giggle. 'A dance, wow; I have to see that.'

He shuffles around on the blanket and waves his hands about, striking feminine poses, and I laugh out loud.

'I'd like to meet your sisters one day, they seem fun.'

Danny rolls his eyes.

'What about you?' he asks. 'Are your parents worried about what's going on in Europe?'

I shrug. 'I guess. Dad is saying he won't have a vaccination if they develop one, Mum is saying she will make him, so I guess that's the main topic in our household right now. It's good to get away.'

Danny chortles. 'I think meeting up like this is good for us both.'

I take a deep swig of my beer to calm my nerves whilst nodding. It is certainly a refreshing change from the jigsaws, the news, and the repeats of shitty sitcoms. Or the family board games, or the endless bickering with Dad.

Meeting with Danny is the highlight of my week.

'So…' I say awkwardly. I watch him grin, like he knows.

'So?' he replies.

I feel my heart rate go wild as he draws me closer to him. Kissing my mouth, touching my body. I forget where we are; I forget about the epidemic sweeping the world. At this moment there is only me and Danny and the sunshine. He lays me back gently, and we embrace.

We meet the next day, and the day after that. I am intoxicated. I think I am falling in love hard, and I am a constant source of entertainment for Emma, who insists on hearing all the intimate details of our secret meetings. She texts me morning, noon and night.

I am pretty sure my mum gets her suspicions that something is happening with me when she hears me singing in the shower and floating around the house like I'm walking on air. Dad couldn't be more oblivious. But giving her credit where credit is due, Mum doesn't ask me questions or try to discourage me from going out. She just asks me to be careful. I give her a small kiss on the cheek.

'I love you, Mum.'

She gets all flustered and gives me a cuddle, kissing my forehead.

'I guess you're not a child anymore, my love, but you will always be *my* child.'

'Always,' I say, and add 'I will be careful.'

She never even chastises me for breaking lockdown rules, and for that I feel a newfound respect, and we seem to have this womanhood, a secret mutual understanding.

For the next three weeks, life is pretty perfect, until I get a text from Danny.

He can meet as usual, but it won't be for long, and may be our last time. He will explain when he sees me. I'm sick with nerves by the time I reach out spot at the top of the meadow.

'Hey,' I call, spotting him where he stands by his bike. 'Is everything okay?'

He seems agitated, and only manages a small smile. Backs away when I come closer.

'It's one of my aunts. She is sick with the virus,' he spurts.

'Don't come any closer to me. I was with her all last night. Called the ambulance, held her to me. I don't want you to get ill.'

'Danny.' I pause, stopping in my tracks. 'I'm so sorry. Will she be, okay?'

He shakes his head, and I see he is tired and emotional.

'I don't know. I don't think so. She could barely breathe. No one is allowed into the hospital, not even my mum. But I think we will find more out later.'

I nod my head, keeping a foot or so apart from him as he wishes, but longing to console him. Hold him.

'What can I do?' I ask weakly, knowing there's nothing, as he shakes his head.

This is it, I think. Real people we know, dying.

His aunt is going to die, he knows it as much as I do. The elderly, obese people, and people with health conditions are starting to drop like flies all around us. The hospital is full, and even nurses and doctors are getting sick. The news last night spoke of converting hotels into places to keep the dying. The supermarkets are running out of supplies because the supply chain is broken, and people are starting to fight over stupid things like toilet roll and bread in the aisles. Breathing or coughing on someone has become a crime.

When I actually think about it, and step out of the Danny bubble, my world, the only world I've ever known, is being destroyed around me. It just hasn't felt real. I've been waiting for it to go away, for the media to say: *'We got it wrong! Everything has been exaggerated, and we can all go back to normal.'* But it's not happening, it's only getting worse: and now this.

'I'm scared, Danny,' I blurt out.

He looks at me with a kind of sad pity on his face.

'I think everyone is scared, Elle.'

I feel my face flush. Like a child that's been reprimanded.

'Does this mean we can't see each other anymore?' I already know the answer.

He nods sternly. 'We have to keep the people we love safe, Elle. What if I get sick now, and pass this onto you, and you pass it onto your parents? They're older, right? Could you live with yourself?'

I avert my eyes, full of mixed emotions and quietly say, 'I guess it's goodbye for now, then?'

He inhales sharply. 'It sucks, Elle. But yeah. I'll text you tonight, huh? Let you know about my aunt. I love you, Elle.'

I stand shocked. He said it. He said it first and I don't know what to do! He smiles, that cheeky, bashful smile he has, his long lashes over his gentle eyes. He's not expecting a reply as I stand dazed on the spot. I watch him put on his helmet and get back on his motorbike. I bite my lip to hold back the tears as he drives away. I don't know why it hurts so much. Everything he said makes absolute sense, and he's just told me he loves me. I should be on cloud nine; I am, but I'm scared. It feels like there's a chance I'm never going to see him again.

Present Day

The little girl is heavier and stronger than I would ever have imagined. It takes a real fight to put her back into the pushchair after checking her over. She is screaming again, and I don't blame her. I would be screaming too if a big wet stranger manhandled me in the rain, then put me back into the place I'd been desperate to get out of, whilst taking me away from my mum.

I glance at the body as we pass and make a silent promise to come back and bury her. It feels cruel to leave, but I am learning my lessons in this merciless new world, and you must prioritise those who are still alive. The dog trots obediently beside me, as I guide us all through the allotment and back out onto the tarmac street that now resembles a turbulent river.

'Ssh.' I hush the baby every so often, whipping my head in all directions. I am so worried we are going to bring unwanted attention our way, and there's a house up ahead, where I know there's another survivor. A woman called Sue. Maggie says she's half-mad and still has the corpses of her family rotting in the upstairs bedrooms, but she is harmless enough. I still stare at her door as I pass. I do not need any extra issues right now. I weave in and out of soaking weeds, broken glass hidden in the downpour, and discarded furniture and rubbish which still litters the streets from the riots, all the while trying to soothe this vulnerable little creature I am pushing around. As I get closer to Maggie's house, I feel my adrenaline start to subside. Warmth, food, and safety await us. I enter the little yard and rap urgently on her door. Waiting.

'What on earth…' she exclaims, her face full of concern as she stares at the pushchair and the dog.

'Her mum is dead. I found them in the allotment. I need your help.'

'Of course, child, bring them in.'

She steps to the side whilst we step clumsily inside together and stand dripping in the hallway. The baby's screams seem much louder now we are out of the rain. With gurgles and spats of deep breaths following each sound, I am sure she will be sick.

'Is she hurt?' Maggie asks.

'I don't think so. I checked her out, but she hasn't stopped crying. I think they've been outside for hours.'

'Poor thing, she's frozen to the bone and probably starving. Right, take her into the back with the dog. I'll get some towels and a coal fire on.'

I stare worriedly down at Maggie as she mops up our droplets with a towel. Images fill my mind of black smoke spiralling out of the chimney for survivors to see for miles around.

'The fire? In daylight?'

'It's a risk, Elle, but she might die if we can't get her warm.'

I nod. We can't let this baby die. I put a towel down for the dog, who settles down gratefully on it, and Maggie rushes in to start the fire with some wood cuts offs and screwed-up newspaper she uses for kindling. I unclip the baby from the harness, taking off her sodden suit, and she starts to settle into exhausted sobs once she's in my arms.

'There, there,' I coo. 'Who's a brave girl?'

Her skin feels so cold when I touch her face.

'The fire is going to take a while to get warm, and she might need her nappy changing, too. Strip her quickly and I'll look to whip something together.'

'Oh,' I say, internally panicking. 'I've never changed a nappy.'

Maggie doesn't look up from the fire, but I hear a smile in her voice.

'You'll be fine, Elle, there's a sponge by the sink. Put the stove on and warm some water.'

I hesitate for a moment but decide on placing the girl on the floor whilst I step over her and rush to turn the switches for the stove. A satisfying click ignites the flames. There's a pan on the top, so I fumble for a water bottle amongst a stack of containers kept on the kitchen counter and pour the contents into the pan.

There's a gurgling noise.

I whip back to see the little girl is toddling around the room, exploring Maggie's knitting. Maggie is watching with amused relief from the fireplace. 'I think she's going to be okay.'

I release a sigh and feel an unexpected lump in my throat.

'Good.'

We spend the next few hours fussing over the girl. Maggie shows me how to clean and redress her with an old cloth she has found as a makeshift nappy, tied with a safety pin. We keep warm by the fire, that heats up the entire house, and we make warm porridge for us all.

'It's good she has teeth,' Maggie says, offering her another spoonful, making airplane noises as she lands the spoon in her giggling mouth. I look blank.

'We don't have milk or baby food, and with her mother dead, she wouldn't survive. Well, unless we scavenged and found some.'

I nod in understanding, looking at this new addition to my life. She wouldn't survive. Maggie is right, and the likelihood is that she won't survive with me. I'm barely surviving myself. It's been about a year since the world as I knew it ended, and I still don't feel any further forward in my knowledge of self-care, or navigating this new lonely, empty world.

'Can she live with you?' I ask hesitantly.

There's a silence I didn't expect. Maggie stands up off the floor, leaving me with the porridge and the girl waiting for more food. The dog looks longingly at us all with frazzled, smelly fur still drying from the rain, its tail wagging frantically.

'That's not a good idea, Elle. You found her. *You* need to learn how to look after her.'

I'm confused. I thought Maggie would have been keen to offer her a home. She offered me a home, why not this baby? Maybe the responsibility is too much? I give another mouthful to the girl, thinking desperately.

'*She can't come back with me. There's nothing for us there.*'

'Okay, how about I move in too, then, like you wanted, and I can learn how to look after her? We can raise her together?'

Maggie smiles, but there's a sadness to her face I can't quite place. After a moment, she nods.

'Yes, okay, Elle. Let's do that, if, you are sure?'

I'm not sure, not sure at all. There are so many anxieties I suddenly have, but I need Maggie for this. My heart races as I find myself nodding, looking at the girl's heavy eyes rolling with tiredness as she lays herself down on the carpet, putting a chubby thumb in her mouth.

There's a strange maternal feeling that shoots through my body. Survival is suddenly not about me anymore. This innocent little child needs people to care for her, to show her how to live in this leftover world. She will have no memories of her mother; she won't understand what the virus was. There are no schools, no medicines, no other children, no supermarkets, no electricity and all the other things I had once. It's just me and Maggie, and our responsibility to help her live.

'Are you going to name her?' Maggie asks suddenly. 'She needs a name.'

'Me?' I laugh nervously, but then I think for a moment. 'Yeah, actually I will.'

I look at her little face, content and happy with us, despite the day she has had. I think of the tiny temper, and the fight in her spirit when I first found her. The infectious giggles she produces. There's only one obvious conclusion.

'I think I'd like to call her Emma. After my best friend.'

Emma settles in surprisingly well, better than I do, in fact. I think both Maggie and I expected—and braced for—a rough first few nights, but they didn't come.

Emma and I share Maggie's spare room, and each night she falls asleep quickly, grabbing my hair. I don't hate it. It's the first real connection I have felt since meeting Maggie, but it's also very different. More intense, more loving. I feel fiercely protective of her already, and she seems to have warmed to me. I think she likes the colour of my hair, as I catch her staring at me often, mesmerised and smiling. I talk to both her and the dog, who I have named simply 'Boy,' in the same singsong manner which they both love. Boy is a thief. We soon learn we must watch every scrap of food we have, or he is straight into it. The first week living together whilst the weather eases off are nice. We sit, cook tasty food, and laugh a lot, watching Emma explore the house. I learn how to clean her and wash the cloth nappy, and how not to feel queasy doing it. Holding my breath helps.

I learn how to rock her to sleep and sing songs copied from Maggie which I have almost forgotten about from my own childhood. Emma loves the singing, so we do it often.

On the ninth day, the rain finally stops, and I remember my promise to Emma's mother. Maggie encourages me, she says it will be good for my soul. Maybe to also go back to my own home afterwards, pack some clothes, along with any food to bring back. Her supply is dwindling quickly with the three of us and Boy.

I agree, taking Boy with me for the walk. I will be glad to pick up some belongings and maybe bring some photos back, too. Boy trots happily with me, I don't put him on the lead, I secretly hope he might be a hunting dog and fetch us a duck or a pheasant, or even a cat. Any fresh meat would be welcome. I crave it. He weaves in and out of gardens, smelling and urinating on every corner and every lamp post. It makes me laugh. I remember a time when dogs were everywhere.

It's a quick walk back to the allotment, and as I approach, I see everything looks the same as when I left it. The gate is closed over with the lock still bust off, and if I squint towards the bottom of the gardens, there's still a body lying cold in the mud. I feel my heart rate rise as I head towards her, grabbing one of the shovels anchored into the soil as I pass. I guess I was half hoping she was gone, and that I was wrong, and she had just been sleeping, but no such luck. Her face faces mine as I approach, milky eyes staring vacantly from bloated, pale skin. Boy distracts himself whilst I bend down over his former owner to rifle through her soaked coat pockets. It's not nice, and I apologise to the body several times. I just want to check if there's anything important in there that maybe I could give to Emma one day. My fingers clasp around something—a little bottle—and I pull it out. It's medicine, baby medicine, in a brown bottle, pink liquid sloshing around inside. I read the label.

'Huh, contains paracetamol. Mild to moderate pain.'
That will be useful, no doubt, for Emma. I pocket it and dive back into the coat. I feel the cold shape of a pen knife and a little book, quickly plucking them from the coat. The book is a passport. Crimson, with elaborate gold patterns and lettering.

'Portugal Passaporte,' I read, flicking through to the back page. It's almost six years old, but the photo of the dead woman is a clear match.

'Gabriella Maria Rocha,' I mumble in my best accent. 'Beautiful.'

I find I am feeling emotional. She was only twenty-five when she died, and my age when this photo was taken. I don't know what she was doing here, although Maggie thinks she must have heard about the trade group on Fridays. At least now I have her date of birth and the approximate day she died; I can give this information to Emma one day. I swallow this weird feeling of grief and concentrate on what I must do. Picking up the shovel, I walk to an unmaintained vegetable patch nearby, where weeds sprawl over the dark soil. I start to dig.

It's hours before I've finished, and I'm happy the hole is deep enough. My arms and back are crippled with soreness, my fingernails black from scrambling around. Boy is asleep nearby after digging up his own holes around the allotment, tired out and pleased with himself after catching and eating some kind of mouse or rat.

I don't waste time dragging Gabriella into her grave; I'm exhausted, and I still have the walk to my house. *Her body is not human anymore,* I think, as I grab her boots and pull. She is frozen in death, like a statue, and every part of her is bloated, stiff and still as she falls into the earth with a sickening thud. As a sign of respect, I reach down and place over her face an old bit of cloth I have found, then quickly begin to throw the mound of soil back into the hole.

It's a shallow grave, but eventually it is done. Sweat rests on my forehead and turns cold quickly with the chill of the winter air. I stick the shovel in the ground and grab one of the bamboo canes I've seen, wrapping some more cloth cut-offs around the shovel to make a cross. I don't know why I've made a cross. I don't think I believe in God, not after humanity has been wiped out by a virus, and after the things I heard the religious nuts did towards the end.

Emma won't learn about religion. I don't know enough about it to teach her, but nonetheless, there's a strange comforting feeling seeing the cross. Like that's how it's supposed to be. I promise Gabriella that in the spring, we will lay flowers and make her resting place look pretty.

'C'mon, Boy,' I call, and we make our way to collect what's useful from my home, to bring to my new life at Maggie's with Emma and Boy.

13 Months Earlier

I stare at the TV, horrified.

Mum and Dad are here with me, and Mum hasn't stopped crying properly in three days. I am lost, numb.

The world has turned into a repulsive horror movie. Everything we have ever known has been turned upside down in less than four weeks. We watch as members of Parliament are dragged through the burned streets of London. I see Westminster Bridge in the background, and the crude, rushed gallows the rioters have assembled on the back of an open armoured truck that overlooks the Thames River.

People are angry. Thousands upon thousands are dying from the virus every day. There are bodies piled up in hotels, spilling out into the street. Mass graves and funeral pyres across the country can't be created quick enough. Hospitals have shut down, replaced with mobile military aid. Fear and anger have turned into blame, and the army can't stop this nightmare, although they have tried. There are bullet holes on every corner in London. Blood stains on every street. The capital has fallen to the rioters.

It's the same in Paris, Berlin, Milan, and even as far as America, Africa and China, as news reporters record the unthinkable. They are as shocked and frightened as us all.

I turn my head away from the TV as they hang another person. There's no censorship on the telly anymore, there's no entertainment, or repeats of dull sitcoms. It's just raw reporting from channels that refuse to shut down.

'Jesus Christ,' Dad swears. 'They've all gone mad!' Dad changes the channel, and it's a different reporter at a vaccine demonstration in Scotland. Hundreds of people all gathered to reject the idea of an experimental vaccine. They are fighting, hitting police, smashing the windows of a laboratory somewhere.

'What if that happens here?' I ask tentatively, about the scenes we've just witnessed. Mum sobs even louder and Dad frowns, as though I've been tactless.

'The army is providing us essential food right now, that's not going to happen here. The cities are full of crazies. Someone will be held to account once this has passed.'

I stay silent.

Dad still believes our isolated little village is going to be safe, and that all this is just going to go away, but he is ignoring his neighbours, who are getting ill. He won't listen to the local

89

social media groups, who update the community about how we can't process any further bodies in the cemeteries, and that we will have to start building communal funeral pyres instead.

He says it is all collective drama.
He has also completely dismissed my grief over Danny and being parted from him. Mum *had* to tell him what had happened after I cried for a week straight.

He has never spoken to me about it, so we pretend Danny doesn't exist. I know Dad is scared, and I do not see the point in arguing with him. I love him, but he doesn't know how to handle his fear, especially in front of me.

'I'll go to the civic centre today,' I say, 'I need some air.'
I pull on my hoodie, grab my backpack, and leave.

The civic centre is a crumbling red-brick council building at the top of the high street. The army is there. They came around a fortnight ago when the supermarkets closed, and they have emergency supplies, medical equipment, and rationed food. You are only allowed three visits a week, and it's a scary place. There are terrifying signs claiming they will shoot you if you cause disruption or are deemed to have the virus and do not leave the premises. You must pass through several vetting processes before you are allowed inside to collect what you need, including a blood test and a swab of your nostrils and throat.

The lockdown got super-serious, super-fast.
But even though I'm nervous about going again, I need space to think. I haven't heard from Danny in two days, and I'm worried. He hasn't been right since his aunt died.

I walk the direct route to town. It's so quiet. No cars are allowed on the roads now, they're just parked outside houses.

You can actually go to prison for driving.
There are also other bizarre new laws, like you must *always* wear a face mask outside your home, but it has never been explained how this disease is spreading so quickly. Only that it's in the air, in people's breath, and a face mask may help you survive. I don't believe in it, but I wear one anyway.

I keep my head down as I walk and try to keep thoughts of Danny away. A few young kids play in their gardens, as brown and orange leaves blow around the roads and paths; the season is changing. As I get closer, I see people up ahead, heading in the same direction through the town and up the steep hill towards the civic centre. There are military vehicles parked everywhere. A few trucks, some 4x4s, and a green cargo lorry, even a tank. I don't understand why they need to bring a tank to give out supplies. It's chilling.

Soldiers with guns roam in pairs around the high street, clearing away loiterers. It's all very intimidating, and I can't take my eyes away from the guns.

I join the long queue. Four big white tents are erected before the building. I keep at least two metres between me and the person in front, and there are blue lines spray-painted on the concrete floor to stand on. We all stand in silence. I read the government signs whilst I wait.

'Keep your distance to save lives'.

'Do not enter if you have any of the following symptoms: Fever, sore throat, runny nose, headache or joint pains'.

'You will be refused entry if you test positive for the above symptoms and will be requested to leave. Anyone refusing to leave the area will be shot'.

I look at my boots until, after what feels like an age, I finally reach the front of the queue. There's no politeness here. They bark orders: where to stand, where to sit. We are ushered like cattle around the tents. First for a blood test, then the swabs. Some of the personnel are in full hazmat suits, some with just masks on, like mine. Every so often there's a cry or a scream when someone realises they have tested positive for the virus.

Testing positive means certain death.

They are refused entry, manhandled immediately out of the tents. No food or supplies whilst you die feels cruel, but why waste good food on someone who won't be here within three days? Because that's how long they're saying it takes from the first symptoms now. Three days.

A tall and extremely serious soldier shouts at me, pointing to a yellow circle on the floor.

'Stand there.'

I do as I'm told and await my results. I know I will either be allowed in the building or quickly ushered away and out of the tent, ordered to go and die at home.

'Good to go!' The soldier barks again, making me jump out of my thoughts.

He points the way to the door, putting a green lanyard around my neck to show others I have been tested. I give a weak smile and head inside. There are more soldiers here, watching, ensuring that everyone only takes the rations allowed from the rows of tables placed out. It reminds me of that last day at college. I open my backpack and walk along the tables picking up our allowance. One bag of flour, a box of twenty silver foil sachets of military stews, hotpots, sausages and beans. They are not bad with a bit of salt.

There are some sachets of fruit-in-juice, a UHT milk carton, two rolls of loo paper, and I can choose between a bag of broccoli or green beans, so I go with the green beans.

It's not a lot. I am thankful there are still a few local people bringing items around door to door, like fresh eggs, homemade bread, cakes and jams.

Happy to get away from the civic centre, I hand back my lanyard and basically run away. My bag straps dig into my shoulders with the weight of my newly acquired supplies, and I enter the high street ready to set back home, when I feel a vibration in my pocket. It's Danny:

'Elle.

My Mum. I don't know what to say. My Mum is dead. I'm in London with my sisters. We came to find our cousins. It's crazy here, but I need you. Christ, I need you. I'll call soon. I love you so much. Danny'

I release a pained whimper, clutching my heart.

'Oh, Danny!'

I am about to call him when there's a sudden screech of wheels and a loud crash and screams from behind me. I drop my phone, then turn to see a van has driven straight into the vetting tents, ploughing down whoever was inside.

'Shit!'

I bend to pick up my phone, not taking my eyes off the scene before me. I am about to go running over to help, when the van door opens. Four masked men jump out, spraying gunfire into the crowd where I have just been standing.

I scream, almost tripping over my own feet as I dive into the shadows of a closed shop, pressing my body up to the steel shutters.

I see a woman grab her child and run towards me. Gunshots echo around, and they shoot them down.

I can't seem to move.

I'm completely frozen with fear, as I watch soldiers return fire and flames begin to encase the civic centre. There's screams, chaos and blood everywhere.

I slip down to a crouching position and bury my head in my arms. When I look back, I see a solider shoot the last of the rioters.

There's a moment where it's silent.

I realise I am shaking as I stare at the place I just walked away from, less than a few moments ago.

Then the screaming and the crying starts.

I try to breathe, looking at the symbol on the van. I realise it has been tagged with rioting propaganda: these are the radical insurgents. The same people from London. The same logo we saw on the news: a needle, with a drop of blood at its tip.

'What happened?' A man has appeared, looking down at me with wide eyes. 'Are you okay?'

I don't answer, I can't.

He holds out his hand to help me up. 'I heard the commotion from the other street, did you come from getting your rations?'

'I, I have to go, and help,' I stutter.

I notice he is staring at my backpack.

'No,' he answers. 'The heat from the flames will beat you back. Give me your bag, and you can go home.'

For a second, I do not register that this is a command. His voice is so gentle.

'Give me your bag, you've just had your rations, right? Give them to me.'

I feel a heat rising in my veins and I stare into his eyes with defiance: is he actually trying to mug me? In the midst of all this chaos?

'No,' I shout, taking a step backwards.

He rolls his eyes and pulls out a kitchen knife from his coat pocket; he is trembling, but with fierce determination. His eyes are wild.

'Give me the rations, or you'll be another body on the road.'

I can barely comprehend what is happening, then another voice roars sternly at us.

'DROP THE KNIFE AND LEAVE.'

We both glance to the side and see the solider who shot the rioter, a face mask still hanging from his chin. He wears a blood-stained uniform, with a semi-automatic pointed at my wannabe mugger.

'Alright, man!' The man who would steal my food drops the knife and holds his hands up in surrender.

'LEAVE!' the soldier screams. The man doesn't hesitate, but as he runs, the soldier fires a single round, tearing him down in his tracks.

I scream. 'Shit! Oh my God! WHY DID YOU KILL HIM?'

The soldier puts his gun down and looks at me with a cold stare. 'I am done,' is all he says, turning to walk away.

There are no ambulances to help the people injured in the attack. No fire service. A few police officers arrive, and neighbouring residents from the houses in town tentatively leave their homes to administer aid and do what they can as the fire turns the roof of the building into a burnt skeleton. I stay to do what I can to help.

After what feels like an age, I walk home in a tearful daze. It's almost dark now and I have been gone hours. Mum is already there to greet me at the door. She sees my ash-covered face from moving bodies and debris. She sees my vacant traumatised expression, and cries out, running to hug me.

To hold me.

I burst out crying, unable to put into words what has happened. I drop to my knees in her safe embrace. At some point Dad joins us, and I feel his arms squeezing around us both. Then for a long time, with no words needed, we just hug and cry. We are all sobbing, standing on our driveway, our hearts breaking. Knowing the world as we have known it is ending, knowing we might all be dead soon, and trying to hold on to each other for that little bit longer.

Despite the horrors of the day, I sleep deeply. I manage, after a hot bath and a mug of hot chocolate, to describe the events to my parents. Then Mum makes up my bed and stays with me holding my hand and caressing my forehead until I fall asleep, like she used to do when I was little. I do not ask her to leave.

It isn't until I wake the next morning, hearing the blackbirds, that I remember about Danny, and my phone. I rush to grab my jeans off the bedroom floor and pull out the mobile. The screen is cracked, but I can still see what I need to:

Six missed calls and four messages from Danny.
Five missed calls from Mum. One message from Emma, and too many friend group messages to pay attention to. I open Danny's messages first, cursing myself for forgetting about him for so long.

'Elle. Call me'

'Elle, are you there? I need you'

'Please Elle, call me when you get this.'

And the last message:

'I don't know where you are? I hope you're okay. We're in London. This is so fucked up. I need you! I love you. Danny.'

'Shit.'

I ring Danny straight away. The phone goes straight to voicemail. I try again. Voicemail. I take a breath and call a final time, ready to leave a message after the flat tone.

'Danny. I'm so sorry. I don't know what to say. I'm so sorry. Something bad happened here yesterday. I couldn't ring you. I need to know you're okay? Call me.'

I hang up feeling terrible. Then I open the message from Emma.

'Elle. I'm so scared. My brother is sick, and Mum and Dad are too. I don't want to die.'

I rub my face with my hands. Everything is falling apart. I can't cope with this.

I spend the day in bed. I have no energy to face anything. Thoughts of the attack spin around and around in my head. Watching the child and mother being killed in front of me. The mugger, desperate enough to try and take my rations, and then losing his life for it because a soldier with a gun had given up on what is right and wrong.

Then the realisation that there is no help. That society is breaking down faster than I can comprehend. I had to watch injured people burn to death because we couldn't help them.

The warmth of my head under the sheets is all that comforts me. I can't help Emma. I want to comfort her, but I don't have the right words. I text her whilst tears fall down my cheeks.

'I love you so much' is all I can manage.

I don't hear back from Danny, either. I send a few texts to him, reading his last message over and over. I call again, but it is still on voicemail. I send a final text:

'Danny, I love you'

By the end of the day, I am truly depressed.

I think I finally understand the soldier. We are all waiting to die anyway, what difference does it make if that man was shot, starved, or caught the virus? What difference does it make if I ever talk to Emma or Danny again? We are all done.

Within the week, news stories circulate of mass group suicides, and mass shootings. Then one by one the TV stations close down, replaced by grey fuzzy static. The last story to air, however, is that the vaccine trials haven't worked.

'This is an extinction event for mankind.'

The army disbands. People quit life. Then Dad begins to cough and sneeze, and I know it is the end.

Present day

Emma and I have lived, quite blissfully, with Maggie for a couple of weeks now.

It's a different type of existence than being in my own home, but not unpleasant; in fact, I am warm, well fed, and feel safe for the first time, in a very long time. Maggie is strong. Not afraid to scavenge through the houses where the dead fester. She has so much knowledge about food and herbs, and just surviving in general. Every day I find I am learning something new. I flick through stacks of her gardening books on how to grow vegetables and am shocked at how easy it sounds. I try knitting. I learn how she has filtered the rainwater from the water tank in the backyard with gravel and sand, so she doesn't have to boil everything. She was made for this life. But there's something nagging at me.

Something not quite right.

I can't exactly put my finger on it, but despite how strong she is, she looks thinner and more fragile every day. Her face looks worn and occasionally pained. If I ask how she is, she gives me a stern look and bats me away like a silly child. Other than my concerns about her health, my only gripe is the trade group.

Every Friday, Maggie leaves the house, taking her shotgun for protection and a shopping trolley with items to trade. Sometimes these items are things she's acquired from scavenging houses. Sometimes she bakes, or cooks things to bring, and I must admit to myself that in a way, her trade group is invaluable. She always returns with useful things like oats, flour, or rice, and has even sourced a baby carrier to put Emma in, like a backpack. We joke about how I can literally wear Emma now.

But every week she asks me to join her at the allotment meets, and every week I say no.
I see how frustrated it makes her, and I am sorry for it, but the thought of meeting with strangers fills me with an inner dread I am not able to verbalise to Maggie.

There has been a meet this morning. I feel sick with anxiety as I wait in the house, pacing up and down the rooms like a caged lion. I don't like it at all. The whole thing feels so dangerous, but eventually I see two figures walking up the grey street, pushing what looks like a gas canister on a wheelbarrow. One of them is Maggie. The other is fair haired man.

I watch through the net curtains in the upstairs window. There's a gun hanging on a strap around his shoulders.

Maggie's shotgun hangs loosely by her side. She looks relaxed as they stop, and she waves goodbye. I watch him give a couple of back glances to the house, that makes my pulse rate rise. Maggie knocks on the door and waits for me to unlock it. I wait longer than is needed.

She greets me cheerfully. 'Hi!'
I usher her and the wheelbarrow in quickly and lock the door.

'All okay?' she asks, navigating around the wheelbarrow as she takes off her coat and boots.

'Mmm hmm,' I reply unconvincingly. 'Who was that?' Maggie pauses, knowing I must have spotted them from the window. I can tell she is choosing her words carefully.

'That was Tom. I've told you about him before. The leader of The Hive. The wheel broke on the trolley, and he offered to push it back for me.'
I remain silent.

'He wants to meet with you. He's not much older than you, you know. Late twenties?'

'That is *much* older than me,' I snort, 'and the answer is still no.'
She ignores my sulking and walks into the kitchen to see Emma. Maggie found her a highchair and toys from a neighbouring house, and she is sat content, playing, strapped

into the white plastic seat whilst Boy lies underneath it at her feet. Expecting crumbs from food, no doubt. She kisses Emma's head and fusses her whilst addressing me cooly.

'Well, I have some news from Tom.'

I roll my eyes whilst I put the metal kettle on the stove to boil for a coffee. I am not interested in hearing anything this Tom thinks.

'The Chosen are growing, and the streets are not safe anymore.'

'The streets have not been safe for ages. He doesn't sound very bright.'

'Okay.' She grins diplomatically whilst wheeling the barrow through the kitchen and lifting off the new canister.

'You are right, in a way; however, Tom says The Chosen have started actively looking for people, like me and you. They call us *easy prey*. People that do not live in groups or communities.'

I blink uneasily, feeling the familiar lump of dread settle in my gut as she continues.

'Tom says there are about six other communities he knows of outside of The Hive, scattered around the country. Maybe even more in the cities, or without communications. The ones he is aware of are all communicating via CB radio, looking to set up some larger scale trade meets, and The Chosen want in'

'Brilliant,' I hiss sarcastically. 'So, what, they're all best mates now, all these communities, Maggie? Including The Chosen, and you're okay with this?'

She sits down at the table and takes the cartridges out of the shotgun, not looking up at me. 'There's more news, Elle, and it's not good.'

I am blindsided, wondering if I have missed the good news, but I say nothing,

'The bad news is that The Chosen want to start trading *people*.'

I stop dead. I can't deny the shiver that has just shot down my spine as I process her words. The kettle starts to whistle, and I turn off the gas, glaring.

'Trade *people* for what?'

She sighs. 'I don't know, exactly, but at a guess: cooking, cleaning, farming the land, maybe to start clearing out the houses and doing mundane jobs?'

There's a stark silence before she looks at Emma and then at me, and adds, 'Women, girls… are always valuable, Elle… for breeding.'

I feel instantly sick, and I rush over to unstrap Emma from her highchair.

'Christ, Maggie. Breeding?'

The terminology makes me want to vomit, and has not only shaken me to the core, but also a terrifying thought has popped straight into my head, if this Tom is talking to The Chosen, he knows where we are right now. He knows we are *easy prey,* as they call it.

'We're leaving,' I spit.

I pick up my rucksack and begin to grab random bits and pieces from around the room as Maggie watches, exasperated.

'Elle, calm down. We are safe here. Safer if we join a community!'

But I am not calm at all. 'Can't you see how this is all a trap, Maggie? *Easy prey,* you said, it can't be easier than you're making it for them.'

She stands up and shakes her head frantically. 'You have it all wrong! The Hive are not The Chosen, Elle! Tom isn't Christopher!'

'Who the *hell* is Christopher?'

I shout louder than I intend, making Emma cry and Boy stand from his spot, confused. Maggie frowns at me as she rushes to hush Emma, speaking in a sing-song voice to settle her again. I take a breath and place my bag back onto the table.

'Sorry,' I mumble.

Maggie smiles sadly and puts a now-pacified Emma down to explore the room, sighing. With my pulse racing, I pour two cups of black coffee, waiting for Maggie to explain everything she knows.

'Look,' she says frankly, 'The Chosen are the worst. We both know that Elle, but they're not going away. They are a strong dangerous pack. They have a primeval, brutal approach to survival, but it's working for them. They are not going to change any time soon.'

She takes a sip of her coffee and sits down on a chair at the table, her eyes searching mine as I stand stony faced.

'Like any community,' She says 'They have discovered they *need* to trade. They need allies, and food, to sustain their way of life. This is where The Hive comes in, and the other communities.'

I grunt 'So, these communities are what? Just accepting the fact that The Chosen have nothing to offer accept weaker people they have taken against their will?'.

'I don't think it's as black and white as that, and many are opposed to it, The Hive are opposed to it. Tom seems to be a good person, Elle, but he has a responsibility to look after his people. They are farmers, like I have mentioned before, but with technology! He tells me they even have electricity! Solar power, with heat and lights.'

I remain silent. Maggie is seemingly trying to impress me by revealing this. I try to keep a neutral expression, even though I feel curious. She takes a breath before continuing.

'So, The Chosen want to start trading with The Hive. They want to learn this technology, and Christopher… Well, he is the leader of The Chosen. He and Tom have spoken, it seems, and have an arrangement that Hive people are off limits. Christopher won't hurt them.'

I sip my coffee for the first time. 'So, you want us to consider joining The Hive?'

'YES!' She smiles. 'You and Emma would be safe. Tom wants you to meet him next Friday to talk, and I said yes.'

My blood is pumping around my body so fast I feel dizzy. Quietly I grit my teeth, but I don't hold back.

'Are you out of your goddamn mind, Maggie?'

I am appalled. I am shocked she is buying into this; she is not only putting me, but Emma in direct danger. I put my coffee down.

'There's something not right with you, Maggie,' I hiss.

'The Maggie I have known for these last few months would never suggest this, the Maggie I know would scoop us up and run and keep running!'

I am staring directly at her, rage and fear combined tingling through my body until she averts her eyes, and then I know I'm right. There's something else going on here and her voice breaks as she begs.

'Elle, you *have* to go to The Hive. It's too dangerous if you don't. I can't protect you. I can't look after you. I thought I could, I thought I'd have more time…'

I instantly soften as tears materialise in her eyes.

'What do you mean, Maggie, *more time*?'

She looks away. Wipes her eyes and sits up straight. 'I have cancer. It has spread, and I will die soon.'

The silence that follows her blunt revelation is haunting. She can't look at me and I'm stunned into silent shock. The only noise that breaks the moment is Emma gargling at Boy, and I have an instant terrified thought. If Maggie dies, I must raise Emma by myself. It's just me and Emma navigating this hideous new world.

'Maggie. Are you sure? Cancer?' I can't hide the panic in my voice. 'How do you know?'

She wipes more tears away and gives a hard smile.

'I had cancer before the virus, it's melanoma. Skin cancer. I was having treatment, and, well, the treatment worked for a time, but it has come back,' she says, matter of fact.

'I tried to cut it out, but it has spread to my lymph nodes.' I want to ask Maggie what a lymph node is, but I feel stupid, so I just listen as she explains how she walked over to see Dr Green last week on the outskirts of town. He confirmed she will only have weeks to live. Not months or years. Weeks. He said she will start getting ill. Really ill. There is nothing he can do to help her. There is nothing she can do to stop it happening.

'This is why you *need* to join a community, Elle, to stay under the radar of The Chosen. A community where other people can help you to survive.'

I am momentarily nettled and brought out of my shock.

'I can survive without the help of anyone else,' I snap.

I'm angry because she hasn't told me sooner. I'm angry because she is dying, but Maggie barks back. It's her turn to raise her voice.

'Really? You can survive without the help of anyone else? I have known you since your parents died, Elle; this last year we have been through *everything* together. You are stubborn, immature, naive, and… lost. You are so lost, and now you have Emma. Do not be selfish as well!'
Every word feels like a stab straight to my heart. My eyes well up and I feel my heart sink even further.

'That's what you really think of me?' I tremble.

'I LOVE YOU, Elle. I need to know you are going to be okay after I have gone.'
I almost choke on the air that I breathe. There's not much more of this conversation I can take. We stare directly at each other in silent acknowledgement, and I nod, wiping my eyes.

'I'm going for a walk, Maggie.' My voice breaks. 'Can you watch Emma, please?'
She sighs and nods sadly, as she watches me grab my bag and leave. I let my legs carry me without thought.

Maggie is dying. My head is whirling with questions I can't answer, and don't want to. There's nothing I can do.

The last person on this earth that cares for me is going to die. I will be left alone to try and keep myself, and Emma alive. When I'm far enough away from Maggie's house, I allow myself to sob loudly.

Our conversation repeats over and over in my mind. Maggie is right, I am lost. Completely helpless again; like last year, when the virus killed everyone I loved.

I walk in and out of dazed hysteria, and at some point, I notice I have let my legs walk me out of the town. I look around at the street I have found myself on. It's one of the newer estates built before the virus. Nice red-top roofs, white garage doors, and paved driveways. I wipe snot away from my face, quiet determination bubbling. I will show Maggie I can change; I can be strong and independent. I can look after myself and Emma without putting us at risk with one of these gangs, or communities that might sell us to the highest bidder. I choose a door and head to it, pressing down on the handle. It is unlocked.

'C'mon, Elle!' I rally out loud. 'Let's do this!'
Maggie knows I hate this; she knows I would rather survive on dandelions than enter the crypts which were once homes.

As always, the unmistakable stench of death casts an instant wave of nausea. I shove my arm in front of my nose to try to shield the smell. The door opens into a dim hallway. Cream painted walls with black-and-white photos hanging everywhere. Light dust and the occasional cobweb cover the surfaces, but nothing extreme, nothing to say people are dead in here. Just the smell.

I take one tiny step at a time, like I am expecting something to jump out at me, but I know this is foolish. Childish, even, and I need to overcome this fear.

My heart races. I push a white panelled door open at the end of the hall. It reveals a beautiful, open-plan kitchen space, a marble-topped island in the middle of the floor, with dirty plates covered in black mould. A quick scan shows there is only the decomposing body of an animal in the corner. Maybe a cat or a small dog. I can't tell. I relax slightly and look around. I see kids' drawings stuck to the fridge with magnets. One is a tiny faded red handprint, and underneath it reads:

'To Mummy. I love you. Ethan age 4'

I try to ignore the lump in my throat as I slip my backpack off and put it on the island, making my way to the cupboards. To my delight, I am rewarded handsomely. They are full! Bags of crisps, biscuits, tinned vegetables, sauces, pastas, and rice. There are even a few cans of lemonade.

I smile, stuffing as much as possible into my bag, working quickly. Maybe this isn't as bad as I imagined. *I can do this.* I can live like this. I will grow things in spring and scavenge in winter. I will show Emma how to survive this way. We will always keep safe and together. I will not put her at risk to the predators of this world.

I walk to the stairs; there may be useful items for Emma in the bedrooms. *'The dead can't hurt me,'* I say over and over, each step creaking under my weight. There's an open door at the top of the landing. It's a child's room. Green and blue tractor wallpaper, and a small bed in the shape of a car.

I see the bodies, and the bile rises instantly. The remains of a mother, on the floor, holding hands with the remains of her small son, their fingers locked together in eternity.

It seems the dead *can* hurt me.

The scream starts in my lower spine and thrusts its way into my chest and throat, finally out of my mouth. I barely register that the sound is coming from me. My knees buckle and I crumble on the top step. I can't stop screaming and staring at the mother and son.

I vomit, as shallow, sharp pants and gasps render me unable to breathe. With a mixture of tears and snot cascading down my face and onto the carpeted stairs, I clutch my chest and try to calm myself, taking in slow gulps of air.

I scream and sob over the unfairness of it all. The lives taken, the people I have lost, and the reality of my life now.

How I will be losing Maggie.

For the first time since the beginning of the virus, I feel like I cannot do this anymore. I can't survive anymore. I won't be able to provide for Emma, I can't live without Maggie.

Darkness overcomes my mind. For a moment, I feel a lightheaded clarity as I scramble back downstairs for my backpack. There's a penknife in there somewhere. I drop to my knees, spilling out the contents over the kitchen floor until I find it. Flicking open the blade, I hold it against my wrist. I throw my head back and scream again.

'FUCK YOU!'

I don't actually know who I am swearing at. The virus? God, maybe? My situation? It doesn't matter. I hold the blade with a shaky hand, pressing just hard enough to make a light cut, but I can't do it.

I am not even strong enough for this.

I throw the knife across the room and lie down on the kitchen floor, curling into a ball. Sobbing with pure self-loathing and helplessness.

12 Months Earlier

There is thirty percent of battery left on my phone.

I am sitting on the end of my bed blinking away tears, looking through the photos of me and Danny, me and Emma, photos of me goofing around with college friends. Photos of my eighteenth birthday only six months earlier.

I will never see these again: in less than a few hours the battery will die, and they will be gone forever.

No gas, and now no electricity. I wonder when the running water will stop.

The house is starting to get cold.

A tear droplet falls on my screen. I am numb, and let it sit there as I swipe my finger to the next picture.

Twenty-nine percent.

I realise I do not have many photos of Mum and Dad, and I hate myself for it. The last one I took of Dad was over a year ago, when we went away for a day trip to the seaside. I am pulling a daft face, whilst we both hold a tray of fish and chips. I feel a sharp pain in my chest, like I am being ripped into pieces. My hands start to shake as I grip the phone tightly, stifling my anguish.

Dad passed away two days ago.

He is in the bedroom next-door, lying-in bed, where I left him, next to Mum. Up to an hour ago, she was still alive, barely. I'm not sure she knows he has died. She keeps calling his name every so often. It's unbearable.

If I'm honest, I don't feel like I even exist right now. Everything is like a dream, like a nightmare. I still expect to wake up each day and find that none of this has been real. That the last six months have been some kind of weird, alternate reality.

If I'm not crying, I sleep a lot, drifting in and out of tormented blackouts, where I am between a vacuum of black abyss and an oblivion of terror. There's no release from this feeling.

When Dad stopped breathing, I tried to call for an ambulance. The phone line was dead. No tone. I ran around in a frenzy to six neighbouring houses, screaming and banging on the doors in panic, until I realised, they were not answering because they were probably dead, too.

Dad is dead. They are all dead.

My memories of the last two days since then are hazy at best. I don't remember eating. I have tried to get Mum to sip water, but she can barely move. Her breathing is raspy, slow, and painful, and I don't want to go back into the bedroom. It's starting to smell of decay already, but I go back in anyway. I need to be there for Mum, so she's not as frightened.

I put my phone down when I hear her call for Dad again, and I walk like a zombie into the darkness of the room. I have closed the blinds and the curtains, turned off all the lights, and I take a seat next to the bed. I hold her frail hand and sing to her. A soothing, melodic childhood song she used to sing to me:

'You are my sunshine, my only sunshine,
You make me happy when skies are grey.
You'll never know, dear, how much I love you,
Please don't take my sunshine away.'

I sing it repeatedly, rubbing the paper-thin skin on her hand slowly, looking at the wall and not at her or Dad. I can't do that; I can't look at them.

Then at some point I hear the same horrible, wheezing sound Dad made. Followed by silence. I try to sing one last verse, but I can't. Instead, I choke on my words.

She has gone.

I bring her hand up to my lips and gently kiss it. 'I love you so much, Mum. I'm so sorry. I'm so sorry.'

Tears track down my face. I sit in detached silence for a while, trying to understand why I'm not sick yet. Mum got sick just after Dad, but I still feel okay. But what if, I think I feel okay, but maybe I am sick, I just don't realise I am.

I put Mum's hand down and leave the room, heading straight for the bathroom mirror. I am shocked when I see myself. Not because I have the viral rash, but because I don't look like me. The me I am used to seeing.

My usual glossy red hair is knotted, and split ends stick out everywhere. My face is ghost-white, and my eyes are blotchy, swollen, and lifeless. I have lost so much weight I am almost unrecognisable, but I am not dying, it seems. Not yet, anyway. I continue to stare at my reflection and odd thoughts begin to manifest. What if I am the only person in the world left alive? What if this is a biblical thing, like all the religious nuts were saying? What if they were right?

Our family are supposed to be Christians, but we are not very good at it. I think the last time we went to church was for a wedding five years ago, but what if I *am* the last person walking on the earth?

This could all be a test of my faith!

I run down the stairs. We have a utility cupboard, and on the top shelf there's an old Bible. I don't think I have ever looked at it. I go to switch the cupboard light on, before I remember the electricity cut out yesterday.

'Shit.'

I run to the kitchen. We have a drawer full of mismatched things and junk items. My heart is racing. I find a candle, fumble carelessly for a match, and strike the box. The flame comes to life with a satisfying crack.

Dad keeps all his tools in this cupboard, but I've seen the Bible somewhere. I hover my new light around the shelves and spot it. Dust-covered, it has not been moved for many years, but I decide I will have to read it. Try and understand why I am not dead, and what I am to do next.

With my parents upstairs, I sit at the kitchen table and flick through the pages. None of it makes sense to me, but about ten minutes into reading bits, I come across a paragraph:
'Now is your time of grief, but I will see you again and you will rejoice.'

I snort loudly. I am not sure I will ever feel joy again. But maybe I will see Mum and Dad again one day; maybe there is an afterlife? One thing I think I know about the Christian religion is that they can't possibly get there, the afterlife, with their bodies decomposing in bed. They should be in a church, have a burial or cremation at least?

I make a decision. I am going to dare to venture back into town. See if everyone *is* as dead as I presume.

See if I can get Mum and Dad cremated, or somehow buried at the cemetery. Leaving the Bible on the kitchen table, I take a deep breath, grab my backpack, put on my trainers and coat, and leave the house. This will be the first time I have left my street since the attack on the community centre.

I walk fast with my head down at first. It feels strange, the streets empty and silent. A different kind of silence than the one lockdown brought.

Surely there must be some people alive?
I walk the main road, which bends and weaves; sometimes it is nothing more than a country lane, until I get closer to town and rows of houses begin to form in a military file. I decide to knock on every door.

'Hello!' I shout hysterically. 'Come out, come out of your house if you're alive!'
The houses and gardens remain unchanged as I run from one to the other, pounding on the windows, rapping on the entrances.

'Hello, if you are ALIVE, come out!' I scream.
I don't think I have eaten or drunk anything for days and it's catching up on me: I start to feel dizzy and sick, stumbling over my own feet, but I won't stop. There's a beautiful detached Georgian mini mansion across the road. The

driveway is as big as my street, and I see the door is slightly ajar. Clumsily running, I careen over the deserted tarmac towards it.

'Hello?'

There's no answer.

'Hello, is there anybody here? I need to know there's someone alive!'

My voice trembles as the wooden floorboards creak under my footing. Still no answer. I explore downstairs. A large clock ticks in the living room, but it's empty in there. I creep slowly upstairs, a musty smell hitting my nostrils as I go.

'Is there anyone here?' I ask quietly now to the returned sound of silence.

What I assume is a bedroom door, made from rich oak, is closed over and I can see the room is in darkness, like my parents' bedroom. The smell is strong now, and I know the inhabitants are deceased in that room.

I pause and decide not to enter. A photograph on a landing mantelpiece catches my eye. An elderly man and woman embracing at the top of the Eiffel Tower. Smiling, full of love and joy. It weirdly makes me smile, despite the situation. I hover for a moment longer and place my hand on the wood.

'Sleep well,' I say to the door and the people behind it.

I walk solemnly back down the stairs and out of the house. My head light and I continue the remainder of the walk into town and towards the cemetery in subdued quietness.

Am I the only person left alive in the world?

When I finally reach the church yard, I find a bench and just sit for a while. The leaves rustle in the breeze over the stone tombstones, and I watch squirrels digging below the trunks. I try not to look behind me. There's a hundred and odd half-cremated, semi-naked bodies stacked in piles, soggy from the night's rainfall. I guess there's nobody left to cremate them.

'Hello?'

The voice makes me whip around in uncertain fear. I leap from the bench to face the woman who called out.

'I'm not going to hurt you,' she says, in a thick, soothing Scottish accent, arms fanning the air as if she's sorry she startled me. I look her up and down. Maybe late fifties, mid-length grey hair, with a few braids knotted in. Her eyes sparkle with kindness, and I start to feel at ease.

'I'm Maggie,' she offers.

'Elle,' I return. 'My parents named me Elizabeth, but I prefer Elle.'

Maggie smiles and takes a step towards me. 'Your parents, are they...'

'Yes,' I answer. 'I came here to see... if I can lay them to rest.' I dare to glance at one of the pyres as my words fail me.

She nods in sympathy. 'Have you been sick?'

I shake my head. 'I had a bad cold a few weeks ago, but it passed quickly. Nothing like the virus.'

She nods again and walks closer with a friendly smile.

'Come inside, we can talk with the others.'

'Others?'

'There's not many of us, but we think, we are survivors. It seems a fitting place to meet, the church, don't you think?'

I shrug, feeling uncertain. Maggie turns towards the medieval stone building, and gestures for me to follow. I see now that the heavy doors are wedged open, and candlelight emits from the gloom inside. I feel nervous, it's a strange feeling to know that I'm not alone after all.

It takes a moment for my eyes to adjust once I'm inside the church. Candles of all shapes and sizes light the giant room, making eerie shadows of the religious artifacts, which dance on the walls. I see a handful of people at the front.

'This is Elle,' Maggie says, introducing me, her voice echoing up to the rafters.

There's a woman sitting on a pew with her head in her hands, crying. She doesn't look up. The rest are men, huddled around a barbecue on the altar, smoke spiralling upwards and out of a window. They all turn to stare, and I feel a self-conscious niggle.

'Fantastic!' shouts one of them, bounding down the steps to meet me. He is a lot older than me but has a handsome face.

'Elle, great to meet you!' He holds out his hand for me to shake. I hesitate.

'It's okay, I haven't got the virus, none of us do. You won't get sick now, I'm sure of it.'

I look at Maggie, confused.

'This is Dr Green,' she says.

'Aaron,' he corrects. 'Aaron Green, I was a doctor, at High Street Medical Practice, did you go there?'

'No,' I reply, 'We were registered at Queens Street.'

Dr Green grins. 'No problem, come sit, eat. Are you warm enough?'

I feel my guard dropping slightly; he is friendly and gentle, Maggie the same. The others, though, have not broken a smile or paid much attention to my arrival. I take a seat at the front of the church and watch as Dr Green goes back to the barbecue. Maggie sits down next to me.

'It's very fortunate we have a surviving doctor, don't you think?' she jokes.

I am a little numb to the irony, so I remain silent.

'He seems a good person, the first survivor I bumped into after I lost my husband. Together we put up posters around town, to tell people to meet today. Did you see those posters?'

I shake my head.

'Oh, well,' she continues. 'It must be some kind of divine intervention you came by today.'

I do smirk at the irony this time.

'Have you eaten lately?'

She looks at me, concerned, and I shake my head. The smell of the meat cooking is almost unbearable.

'Right, well, we can change that. Mr Fletcher over there brought us two chickens plump and plucked, ready for the grill. There's enough for everyone.'

A stocky man with a flat cap gives me a side nod as he stares intently at his cooking, prodding the meat with a fork. The others are standing around him. An elderly gent talking wildly to a large man with an enormous orange beard, and a man who I think is Sikh or Hindu with a large turban on his head is staring up at the stained-glass windows. His clothes are torn, dirty and creased, like he has slept in them for weeks. I imagine I look the same as I notice a hole on the knees of my jeans. I turn to look at the crying woman, who Dr Green is trying to appease.

'Is she okay?' I ask Maggie.

'No, I don't think she is okay. I'm not sure any of us are okay though, really, Elle. I think we are just trying our best to cope right now.'

I nod and decide I really like Maggie.

Over the next hour or so the chicken is cooked and shared around on paper plates. There's also a vegetable soup that Maggie has brought, which she warms up on the dying embers. I have almost forgotten what food tastes like, especially meat. My mouth waters as I savour each slow bite and each swallow of the succulent flavours. By the end of eating, my stomach is satisfied for the first time in ages, and I am ridiculously tired, as though the food has been a sedative. I listen to various stories and conversations of their own fight for survival, and learn that Morgan, the big man with the orange beard, will be heading west on his bike to a farm his family owned, where he knows the fields are fertile, and where the silo will be full of seed to plant in spring. He has a rifle, stolen from a dead soldier, and he knows how to track deer. A small part of me wants to go with Morgan.

I have decided that Timothy Fletcher, with the flat cap, is a scary man. He boasts how he has taken over a factory at the bottom of town; he put Alsatians in the complex, and they are all well fed. He doesn't elaborate, but he says he talks to other survivors on CB Radio, and he will be inviting them to meet up; if they try to steal from him, he will release the dogs.

Maggie talks about her husband, Jeff. How he was her rock, and that she knows he will be watching and willing her to survive. I sit looking at the floor whilst they talk.

One word niggles at me. *'Survivor.'* They all speak as though this virus is over. That a new life is beginning. I can't quite understand it all, so I speak up the next time the great chapel goes quiet.

'The last news report I saw, before the television went offline, said that this virus was an extinction-level event. Nothing could stop it. Nobody could outlive it. The vaccine didn't work, and the mutations were airborne. Are we really survivors? Or are we just still, waiting to die?'

There's stark silence. Then Dr Green stands up before us all, a weird half-smile on his face.

'Excellent question, Elle. I have my own theories, and if you will all indulge me, I would love to share them?'

Nobody speaks, so Dr Green takes this as a cue to elaborate.

'So, the virus is a bacteriophage.'

We continue to stare at him. The word means nothing.

'Okay,' he continues. 'A bacteriophage is a virus that infects a bacterium and uses it to duplicate itself by reproducing inside it. Usually harmless, actually, research suggests, it could have been an asset to human life. Every single person on earth has bacteriophages living inside them. A microorganism, if you will. They are everywhere living things exist. Billions are on your hands, in your intestines and your eyelids right now!'

We all shuffle in our seats uncomfortably.

'However, an extreme curve ball has been thrown. The bacteriophage somehow evolved - the chances, slim - but the mutation was prevalent, catastrophic, and instantaneous. A vaccine would have never worked.'

'Then how are we alive?' I ask.

'That's a good point,' Dr Green answers. 'But I imagine it's because our bodies have something inside that stopped the bacteriophage from spreading. You were sick, right? Everyone was sick at some point?'

We all nod.

'That was the 'virus',' he says, using air quotes. 'That sickness was the same virus that has wiped out the rest of the human race. But I believe we have immunity. I can't tell you why, that would take decades of research.' He laughs. 'But I can tell you, for us, it's over. We are not going to die from it right now. But of course, we can't be certain it won't get us in the end if it mutates again. We can only carry on, trying to live.'

I'm trying to process everything; I look to Maggie for clarification. She just shrugs.

'Hey, that will do for me,' she says, standing up. 'Let's live whilst we can, eh? And in the meantime, let's try and give our loved ones a decent send-off. Elle, these guys have offered to try and cremate the rest of the bodies out there. There's plenty of dry combustibles and fire lighters still in the church outhouse, and I have diesel left in my van. I can drive you home, and come with you if you like, to get your parents' bodies?'

'Thank you' is all I can manage.

Present Day

It is almost a month since Maggie told me she was dying. She has missed the last two trade meets, her health deteriorating quickly. The days go by in a whirl and are long and stressful. I see how little time she has left now she has barely enough strength to raise her head from her pillow. I try not to sigh, or act exasperated around her bed, but constantly cleaning soiled sheets, taking care of both Maggie and Emma, and feeding us all is hard, really hard.

'Is it Friday?' she asks me weakly as I finish propping her up for her morning coffee. 'Will you go? For me?'
I can't help but feel annoyed. It is Friday. She's been keeping a mental note. There's nothing wrong with her marbles, that's for sure. I inhale and look at her, frail and in pain.

'You know I won't, Maggie.'
She closes her eyes and nods, and I take this as my cue to leave. Downstairs, Emma is sleeping, wrapped up in her blankets in the cot. I desperately need to go and scavenge food. We are down to one meal a day as supplies are so low, but the streets are too dangerous. The trade today will bring The Hive, maybe even The Chosen, and whoever else to town, so I begin to peel carrots, ready to make soup for later. I

have propped the shotgun up by the front door. Loaded. I won't take any chances today.

I have only been standing by the table for ten minutes when there's a small knock at the front door. I freeze.

Boy jumps up from his cosy nest of blankets to deliver a low growl. I stop, startled by the unexpected noise.

'Ssh,' I whisper over at him as my pulse begins to race. The knock comes again, a little louder, and this time Boy barks. Emma is woken with the commotion and begins to cry. If they didn't know someone was here, they do now.

'Shit.'

I sprint down the hall and grab the shotgun, checking all the locks are in place, before backing away, pointing it directly at the locked door. The weapon is heavy and shakes in my arms. A muffled voice speaks.

'Elle. It's Tom, from The Hive. Can we talk? How is Maggie?' he asks.

Emma's cry gets louder from the kitchen. I feel a sudden pressure rain down on me.

'Elle, I know Maggie is sick. She told me everything. Please open the door.'

'Go away!' I scream. 'I'm pointing a shotgun at you, go away and I won't shoot!'

For a moment, there's silence. Then a noise from the kitchen, a tap on the window, and looking straight back down the hallway, I see a tall man in a cowboy hat, peering in. I whip my gun around to the kitchen window as Tom speaks again.

'That's Ant, with Kasper in the backyard. We don't want to hurt you, Elle. We want to see Maggie. And you, and the baby.'

I run. I sprint fast and ignore the images of the two people who now stare at us. I grab Emma with one arm as Boy continues to bark, and I dash up the stairs with the gun in the other arm as glass smashes behind us. I dive into Maggie's room, slamming the door behind.

'Elle, what's happening?' Maggie cries, trying to sit up.

'Shit, Maggie, it's your *friend* Tom. They are here for us.' I shrink into the far corner with Emma, pointing the gun unsteadily, and I accidently squeeze the trigger in my panic. It bursts loudly from the gun, deafening me, and blasts a hole into the top corner of the room by the door as plaster rains down. Emma screams and the ringing in my ears is sharp.

'Christ on earth! Give me the gun, Elle,' Maggie commands, finding the strength to hold herself up. I hesitate but she repeats sternly.

'Pick up Emma and give me the gun.'

I feel sick, unsure what to do, but as I hear the footsteps approach and the voices speaking from the staircase, I lose all confidence in myself, and I hand Maggie the gun. She steadies herself and aims it at the door. I pick up Emma, holding her tightly, putting my hand on her cheek to try and soothe her. Eyes wide, I wait for the bang as the door opens slowly. It doesn't come.

'Elle. We're not here to hurt you,' comes the smooth voice as he walks in. 'Don't shoot.'

Maggie holds the gun shakily as Tom takes in the scene before him, his companions hovering behind.

'Maggie.' He grins. 'I'm so happy to see you. I thought the worst.'

I stand, horrified to see Maggie lower the gun.

'This *is* the worst,' she says. 'This is *worse* than death.'

He nods seriously and looks over at me and Emma.

'Elle, I'm sorry. We didn't want to frighten you, but we made a promise to Maggie to keep you safe after she has gone.'

'Fuck you!' I spit.

He gives me a boyish grin and smooths back his blond hair.

'Maggie told me you have spirit, that's what we need in our community, you know, you'll be a great asset.'

Maggie looks to me, her eyes steely, determined, defiled of all emotion.

'Elle, it's time for you to go with Tom. Start a fresh new life. Mine is over.'

She looks at the gun, sighs, then looks back at me, and in a horrifying moment I know her intention.

'Maggie. No!' I shriek. 'Don't you do this, Maggie!'

'I love you, Elle. Know I love you.'

Tom walks over to me and puts a hand on my shoulder.

'Please, Elle, it's time to go.'

I brush his hand away, as he nods to the others. They come straight over and prise Emma from my arms as the wannabe cowboy restrains me. I wail, scream, and kick out, but he's much stronger than me.

'Don't touch her!' I scream in my frenzy. 'Maggie, make them stop!'

But she doesn't. She just grips the gun, looking at Tom.

'Your word, Tom?'

I see him take her hand and nod before I'm dragged down the stairs. I'm grateful for Boy as he goes berserk. Barking and biting at trouser legs as they usher Emma and me outside.

I scream Maggie's name over and over again.

The man releases me at the same time an earth-shattering blast comes from inside the house. A shrill howl I never knew I could make, rises from my throat as I process what she has done. I feel like I've been punched in the gut, dropping to my knees in despair, the world crumbling around me.

'Maggie!' I wail, retching. 'Oh, Maggie! NO, please no!' I put my hands on the cold street and start to claw at the concrete as I kneel and sob in the drizzle. It is almost as if time has stopped completely, and the world is no longer turning. Emma's cries seem distant, and I see only a blur of colours through my despairing, hazy vision.

Tom crouches beside me whilst the other two stand over, Emma frantically squirming to get out of their arms.

'I promise you: it's going to be okay, and I'm sorry you had to lose her like that, but you have to believe me, it's what she wanted.'

I swallow as my tears fall onto the ground, anger rising like a fire inside me. I want to hurt him. I want to hurt him badly.

In the bedroom, I'd noticed he has a big knife, strapped into a brown leather holster on his thigh. The red mist takes over. Before he can react, I push him off balance and reach for the knife, pulling it out. Unprepared, Tom falls onto the street as I plunge it down hard, meaningful, with a great roar. He rolls out of the way just in time and it misses.

'Holy shit!' he yells as I bring the knife down again, but my arms are blocked by the aspiring cowboy. He is strong and rough and doesn't hesitate in almost breaking my wrist to release the knife, as I try to slash at him too.

'Jesus Christ,' he shouts, 'She's feral!'

I hear Tom speak over my screams as he picks himself up.

'Look, Kasper, give her the baby. Ant, just let her go.'

He does, and I calm instantly when they hand Emma back to me. The one with the hat, Ant, glares at me and whips out a handgun from his deep jacket pocket, aiming it straight at us.

'I won't hesitate,' he huffs, 'if you try any of that shit again.'

I shut my wet eyes and squeeze Emma tightly, breathing in her smell as we cling to each other. When I open them again, Tom is staring at me, his grin gone.

'Elle, this doesn't have to be difficult. I know it's been a long time since you had to put your trust in strangers, I get it. Maggie told me everything.'

'Don't mention her fucking name,' I bark. 'Don't talk about Maggie to me!'

He nods. 'Okay. I won't, but you must know. This is her wish. This is for the best.'

I seethe in silence; aware the gun is still pointed at me and Emma. So, I say nothing as he tries to engage with me.

'I'm going to tell you what happens next, okay?' In about five minutes, some more of our people are going to come up this street, and we are making a long, and quite inconvenient journey,' he adds. 'To another tribe. A group called The Chosen, where we will trade items.'

Adrenaline shoots through me.

I was right. I was fucking right.

'Before we go, is there anything you need from the house?'

I hesitate. There's a lot I need. I need things for Emma, I need warm clothes, she hasn't got her jacket. I haven't got mine. Her favourite toy, food. The photo of my parents.

Maggie, I need Maggie.

I feel my heart break all over again but fight the feeling of falling apart in front of these people. My stubbornness and pride take charge and I shake my head defiantly. Tom said this doesn't have to be difficult, but I intend to make it as difficult as can be. I hear him sigh, as the sound of horse hooves fills the street.

'Right, well. We can sort things for you later.'

We watch as a horse and cart trundle up the street, along with another horse leading a cow on a long rope. There are also two goats tethered to the cart, which is full of stuff, and I notice the people leading the animals are female. A dark-haired woman sits on the cart, and a hard-faced blonde woman on the horse. Her eyebrows raise in surprise at Ant when she spots the gun he is pointing at me and Emma.

'It's necessary.' He defends himself before she speaks, and I see a smile cross both their faces.

'Get on the cart, you sit with Kasper,' Ant instructs me darkly, putting the gun away and pulling himself up onto the back of the horse behind the blonde.

Tom's boyish grin has returned, and he waits to make sure I am steady on the cart with Emma and Kasper. We sit nestled in between barrels; boxes; a few cages of chickens; and baskets of fresh food, like apples and carrots. Boy—who has also calmed from his brief outburst now—follows, sniffing curiously at the goats and between the legs of the horses.

'Okay, let's go,' Tom says, catching my eye, attempting to throw me a smile, but I look away. Instead, I focus on Emma as she rattles the chicken cage with delighted wonder, and I glance sadly at the upstairs window of the home we shared together, swallowing away stinging grief. It feels surreal.

Maggie is gone.

Tom climbs onto the seat at the front of the cart, next to the woman who passes him the reins, and we set off. I'm quick to learn this is a hideous way to travel. In the back, we feel every pothole, rock, and bend, thrown about with such force. It costs me all my balance and core strength to hold onto Emma and keep myself upright at the same time.

'Do you…need… any help?' Kasper asks tentatively after watching me struggle for a while. He speaks broken English, and I can't quite place the accent, *maybe Polish,* I think. He looks only a little older than me, and I find myself feeling more at ease with him than I do with Tom or Ant.

'It's okay,' I answer quietly. 'It's just uncomfortable.'
He smiles and nods sympathetically. I notice he has a few missing teeth.

'I am sorry for maybe frightening you? Here, give apple, for the baby, if she hungry.'
He points to the baskets of produce, and despite myself, I give a small smile.

'Thank you.'

Several very uncomfortable hours pass by.

I take up Kasper's offer, keeping Emma supplied with fresh foods, and find myself cursing my stubbornness as the evening air begins to chill my skin and hers. Every so often, I glance over to the horse that follows closely behind. Ant and the woman are in deep, serious conversation. They look like they are in love, the way he holds her tightly, his arms wrapped over her body, leaning in, and whispering close to her ear. Tom's bubbly voice breaks my train of thought.

'Hey,' he chirps.

I turn my head and see he has relinquished his responsibility of overseeing the cart, by handing the reins back to the woman so he can turn around to us.

'It's bumpy in the back. Sorry about that. Is she okay?' He nods to Emma, and I glare back spitefully.

'Why would you care? You're taking us to *them,* The Chosen. To trade us? For what, magic beans?'

Tom stares at me longer than he needs to with that stupid grin, and replies.

'I'd expect a fully grown beanstalk, with a box of gold at the top if that was the case!'

The woman next to him elbows him harshly, and he laughs.

'Shit, sorry. Elle, this is Aisha. She's here to make sure I behave.'

Aisha gives a quick wave, and I turn aside, feeling almost bashful.

'Up on the horse is Sarah, and… you'll grow to love Ant, I promise.'

I glance at them both again, not feeling so sure.

'Have you eaten?' He gestures to the celery stalks and carrots. 'Take some, honestly. You must eat. Hopefully, Christopher will have something ready for us when we get there, but I won't hold my breath.'

At the mention of the name Christopher, anger flushes my face, and it must show, as he changes his direction of babble.

'Maggie said you found Emma at the allotment where we meet for the trades? And you buried her mother there. I've seen the grave,' he says. 'Really honourable of you, I mean it. These kids need us. We've a few orphans knocking around The Hive, you'll get to meet them.'

I raise an eyebrow and look at Tom properly for the first time. Could Maggie have been right? That these people are *kind*, that there is no ulterior motive?

Tom tires of trying to get me to interact with him, and he sighs turning back around. He's clearly upset with how things have panned out with me, but I can't care right now, not when Maggie is dead because of him.

143

It's around another hour, and dark by the time Tom leans into the back of the cart again, seeing Emma asleep across me.

'We are almost here,' he whispers seriously. 'Keep quiet, and no eye contact. These are bad people.'

'I know,' I hiss back. 'So I don't understand what the hell we are doing here.'

Loud enough for both me and Tom to hear, Sarah has leant forward on the horse. 'Me neither.'

I am instantly taken aback by her support, as Tom turns around in a huff. Through the darkness, I see her body language change. Fear.

We approach giant metal gates, bringing the animals and cart to a halt. A flashlight suddenly aims its beam at us, and the sound of guns being loaded springs up from the gloom.

'Whoa, fellas, my name is Tom, from The Hive. Christopher is expecting us.'

My grip on Emma tightens as the gates open to the large stately home's grounds. I watch as our entourage, along with the cow trailing behind, pass two armed men who close the gates again. Turning my head, I spot a mansion up ahead with lights—not candlelight or fire, but electric light—beaming out from some of the downstairs windows, and I can hear music. Loud, rancorous music, above laughter and jeering. It has been so long, I had almost forgotten what music sounded like, but instead of filling me with wonder and awe, I feel a terrified knot in my stomach. The others must feel it too, as Ant grunts in a dissatisfied whisper, as we wind our way along the long driveway and toward the lion's pit:

'Christ, Tom, are you sure about this?'

'Just keep calm, okay. Don't make eye contact, don't rise to anyone trying to goad you. Sensible, calm. You okay, Sarah?'

'Just perfect,' she snaps.

And then we are silent until we reach the courtyard, where we are greeted with around five or six men sitting on stone steps amongst a horde of motorbikes and quads. They are fully armoured, each wearing that same black jacket with the upside down cross drawn in white on the back. This is the heart of The Chosen, alright.

One of the guys stands and flicks a plug switch to turn off the music as the cart is brought to a stand. The hum of a nearby generator fills the new thorny silence as they gather around. Kasper jumps off the cart, helps me down, and I shuffle Emma to rest with her head over my shoulder; thankfully, she stays asleep. I watch Tom climb down from the cart and come face-to-face with a giant of a man. He's a lot older, with a large grey beard. He towers over Tom.

'Christopher is expecting you. I assume the beasts are for us?'

'Yes, except the dog and horses. The other animals need resting and feeding. Where is he?'

There's a chuckle from one of the other men.

'Resting, with his own beast.'

They all laugh. The big guy strokes his beard.

'I'll take you to where you can let up.' He stares too long at Sarah, then gives a cold smile. 'Keep your women close to you if you want to keep them safe.'

Ant jumps down off the horse to stand next to Sarah, and if looks could kill I wouldn't like to place odds on The Chosen right now, but his reaction only causes amusement.

'Follow me then, ladies.' The man chuckles as he leads us all up the steps whilst Tom exhales beside me. I have a desperate feeling that this is not a very well laid out plan.

We enter the building, in awe of the 18th-century stone pillars which reside on each side of the doors. It reminds me of a museum, but the beauty stops as soon as we step inside. It has been utilised as a hub for The Chosen for far too long, and there's an instant musty smell of smoke, sweat and food. Discarded bottles and empty tins lie strewn around the floor, amongst piles of unwashed clothes. There are several rows of bunk beds in the main hallway, which are set before a once-magnificent staircase, over twenty beds. The occupants of this prison-esque layout are scattered around the room: playing card games, lifting weights, all under the glare of florescent lights hooked up to an outside generator. The stark light illuminates graffiti-covered walls; graffiti that has desecrated oil paintings and tapestries, reflecting in a shattered chandelier above our heads. To the right of the room, an enormous open fireplace with steel pots, pans, and a spit roast with a fresh deer carcass that dangles over the unlit pit. It's a sight to behold and a million miles away from the tiny life I've been sharing with Maggie.

We are led directly through this bizarre sleeping area, and I feel curious eyes boring into us, so I nestle my head into Emma's, looking at the floor and watching Boy trot loyally at my feet. We pass through two thick oak doors and are guided to a small, dark and empty room towards the back of the manor house. In the candlelight I can see it has luxurious red walls and gold patterns and emblems on the ceiling. I imagine it was once a study or a library, but whatever books adorned the many empty shelves have all disappeared, probably used as fire fuel. The bearded guy throws an ugly smile, passing over some unlit candles for us to light.

'Stay in this room, Christopher will be down when he's free.'

'Has he not got food for us? Beds? We've brought the items he wanted and have come a bloody long way, with extra supplies for the trouble,' Tom protests.

'I'm sure he appreciates it. I'll let him know about the food. Stay here.'

The door shuts and we are left alone. Sarah, Ant, and Tom begin a whispered argument as we pass around candles. It's clear Sarah doesn't want to be here, and that Tom has had to persuade them all. Boy wags his tail and lies down, exhausted from his long walk, and I go and join him. Sitting quietly in a corner, I place Emma on the floor as she starts to stir, blinking in the strange new surroundings.

'Hello, sleepy head,' I coo.

Then I smell her. I did not bring a change of clothes, or any spare cloth nappies. I internally curse myself and my stubbornness once again, and Maggie's words about *'not being selfish'* sting in my memories as she starts to cry. I yell louder than the whispered argument.

'Emma needs things that I don't have for her.'

The three of them stop immediately and turn their heads. Aisha, who has been standing silently, walks over to us, a kind smile in her warm eyes. She bends down and begins to distract Emma by playing peekaboo.

'Why didn't you bring her things?' Ant snaps.

'At what point?' I retaliate bitterly. 'The point where you manhandled me away from my home? Or the point where you let Maggie kill herself?'

'From what I remember, you were thinking straight enough to almost kill Tom!'

'For God's sake,' Sarah interjects. She gives his chest a light punch and walks over to me too. 'What can we do?' He says nothing more, removing the cowboy hat whilst scowling. I hadn't expected Sarah to empathise with me, being that she and Ant are so obviously together, and he is not my biggest fan, but she seems just as kind and concerned as Aisha.

'She needs cleaning, for a start,' I mumble.

Sarah turns to Tom. 'You need to talk to him.'
I assume *him* means Christopher, and I watch as Tom throws his head back and groans in displeasure.

'Hey, I didn't ask to come with you!' I bark, annoyed by his body language.

'I know,' Tom replies. 'It's fine. I'll talk to him, but when he comes to *us*, okay? I don't want to piss him off.'

We are trapped in this little room for hours. It's cold, dark, and suffocating all at the same time, and the undertone beats from the music and the chatter in the main hallway vibrate around the walls. Emma is having an almighty tantrum. Nothing I can say or do to soothe her works, her cries must be echoing around the entire mansion, and it begins to stress us all out. Aisha and Sarah rally around trying to help pacify her as we engage in clapping games and as much distraction as possible. Finally, after what feels like an age, the door opens.

'Jesus Christ, Tom. You had to bring a fucking brat?'
I flinch. This is clearly the infamous Christopher. He is tall, like Ant, but has a much bigger, intimidating frame. Tattoos are etched into all parts of his skin, reaching up his neck and onto his shaven head. He has a trimmed blond beard, and piercing blue, menacing eyes.

'Sorry,' Tom mutters, standing up like a scolded child. 'Couldn't be helped.'

'Well, bring it in, little cousin. It's been too long.'
My stomach flips as I watch them embrace. Cousins? He looks over at me.

'What's wrong with it?'
Tom answers for me. 'We don't have any food and clean clothes for her. She needs baby stuff.'

'She needs to shut up, it's giving me a headache. Why the fuck would you bring a baby here without its stuff, Tom?' Christopher looks me up and down, I must look dishevelled, scared. He smiles.

'Ah, you've picked this one up with the baby today, eh? One of your vagabonds?'

'Something like that,' he stutters, and changes the subject quickly. 'So, have you seen what we have brought you on the cart? Is it up to expectations?'
Christopher pulls a cigarette and lighter from inside his jacket and lights it, offering one to Tom, who refuses.

'It's good,' Christopher says, 'but why didn't you bring Justin?'
I see Sarah exchange a nervous glance with Ant.

'He doesn't want to come, Chris, you know this.'
Christopher nods. 'But I didn't *ask* Tom. I didn't fucking ask. Douglas told you at that trade meet-up last week, that I specifically said to bring… Justin.'

'Chris, look. I can't *make* Justin come.'
He blows a smoke ring into Tom's face.

'*But I can.*' There's a dangerous pause. 'Is that what you all want? You want me to turn up at your farm and make Justin come with me? I thought we had an alliance. An understanding?'

'Chris, just give us time, okay?'

Emma's cry is the only sound as Christopher puts his face close to Tom's.

'I'll give you time, cousin. Don't fucking disappoint me.' Tom looks at the floor and nods.

'Okay, then.' Christopher claps with a forced joyful laugh.

'Let's get you folks some home comforts; as my guests, I'll make sure you get the very best. Stay away from my soldiers, they're not all as nice as me, but we have full amenities here, and you'll find a range of Portaloos out back, and a clean water tank for refilling bottles. Tom, follow me. Oh, and Sarah, nice to see you again.'

He gives a wink and leaves, with Tom following like a lap dog. There's a tense moment before Sarah hisses at the door as it shuts behind them. She has tears streaming down her face and is shaking. 'I'll slit his fucking throat.'

Aisha stands up, taking her in a tight hold, swiftly followed by Ant, and I have no idea what's going on.

Ten Months Earlier

It's almost spring, but the early morning air still has that cold bite to it. I lie in my sleeping bag on the sofa staring at the window, curtains open, watching the sunrise. I realise I haven't eaten in almost three days. I'm thirsty and starving. I haven't slept properly, either, or washed myself, or done any of the chores I've tried to tell myself I have to do to survive. I try to give myself simple commands to rouse myself into action, like: *'Boil water, Elle. Get a fire going. Move, for Christ's sake.'*

Instead, I close my eyes, annoyed with the inner voices. Waiting to die. The taps stopped working weeks ago. I've been walking to the river to collect what I can in containers I have scavenged, but I refuse to drink river water without at least sieving and boiling it first. This simple action is an arduous task. To boil the water I need to light a fire, to light a fire I need to find fuel to burn, and so on and so forth.

Since helping me cremate my parents, Maggie has asked me twice to move in with her. We have met on a regular basis, but I don't want to leave my home, even though I don't like to go upstairs anymore, or go near my parents' bedroom. This is still my home. This is where I feel safest.

I feel that Maggie thinks I'm pretty useless, like a child, but I'm almost nineteen. I need to learn how to do things for myself, even though I know my stubbornness boarders on stupidity.

My stomach growls loud enough for me to hear it, and painful enough to make me move. I need to eat. There's nothing left in the house. I need to think about scavenging. I will literally be happy to eat cold sardines if I find them, which I hate. I slip out of the bag and walk over to the last bottle of clean water. It's a 500ml water bottle I have reused several times. I swig half of it straight away and leave the second half for later. Feeling exhausted, I force my feet to take me outside, and I stand on our drive looking at the neighbours' homes. I have not brought myself to venture inside them again; I can't. But I knew this day would arrive, the day where all the food runs out and I must make a plan.

So, I have done.

I have a different idea. I am going to catch something. I am going to catch something like a rabbit, or a pheasant. There's plenty of wild animals around. It didn't take them long to realise people had all but disappeared, and now it's spring, the world seems full of life. Only yesterday, I saw a fox in my street.

I watched a survival TV show last year and the people on it used a thin piece of wire to snare things. Dad had wire, so I set up two snares on a country lane nearby, and I have my hammer. That will be the hard bit. Killing it. As I get near to my first snare, the weight of disappointment shrouds me. Empty. It clearly hasn't worked. The second snare, only a few hundred metres beneath a blackberry bush down the road, is the same. I scream in rage, throwing down the hammer, watching the birds scatter around me.

'Okay.' I breathe. 'It's okay.'

But I know it's not, I know I am pathetic and starving myself to death. I can't afford to wait any longer, and I am against rummaging through dead neighbours' cupboards again. So, I decide I will walk to Maggie's house. I pack away the hammer and head towards town, frustrated and defeated.

Maggie is home. I hear her shuffling around inside. She opens the door with a smile.

'Come in, Elle. How are you?'

I shrug as I walk into her kitchen. 'Okay, I guess. How are you?'

I notice she has some boxes of medication on the table that she quickly removes to make space. I don't want to pry.

'Have you eaten today?' she asks. 'I have some porridge and cinnamon on the go.'

Tears spring to my eyes in relief, but I don't want her to see, so I turn and try hard to keep my voice steady.

'Yes, that sounds great, thank you. If you don't mind.'

'No, not at all. We all must help each other out. You remember Mr Fletcher, from the church? Well, I saw him yesterday and he's trying to fix an old radio, hoping he might be able to find other survivors or something, and talk to them. We swapped some supplies and I said I'd keep my eye out for some special batteries he needs. That's the future, Elle. Working together.'

I nod, barely able to take in a word of what she is saying, staring at the bowl she pours the oats into. Finally, after it has cooled enough to eat, I savour every mouthful, trying not to shovel it in too quickly.

'I tried to catch a rabbit in a snare I made. It didn't work. I wondered if you have any books, or tips on catching animals like this?'

Maggie laughs. 'No, unfortunately I don't, but I do have a shotgun which might be a tad easier than using a snare.'

'A shotgun?'

She nods whilst clearing up.

'It was Arthur's, he enjoyed hunting a bit when we were younger. It's been in the attic for years. After he died, I fished it out, along with some cartridges. The thought did cross my mind as well, but I'm not sure how good an aim I am. In fact, how about we hit two birds with one stone? We have a walk to the library, see what books we can find that might help us both out with surviving this mess, and take the road down towards the river afterwards? I always see deer and hare by the bankside at this time of year.'

I practically beam with joy.

'Yes, please!'

'Okay.' She laughs. 'But first, look what I found!'

She goes to her kitchen cupboard and pulls out a large Tupperware box. A treasure trove of chocolate bars, jelly sweets, and crisps.

'I was exploring some houses yesterday. Go on, choose something!'

I know it's silly, but I feel a lump in my throat as I grope through the box, some of my all-time favourite treats, which I haven't had—or even seen—in months! I smile widely as I choose a large bar of chocolate with nutty pieces in, scrambling to get the first bite into my mouth. Both my mum and I used to love this chocolate, and I savour the flavour, closing my eyes. I feel happy. Okay, it may not be *happy* in the traditional sense, the way I used to be happy, but it's definitely some kind of positive emotion.

We pack a few bottles of sterile water, some potato cakes she has made us to snack on, along with carrot and celery sticks. Then there's a knife to apparently remove the guts, some rope, a hand saw, and of course, her shotgun. I am kind of relieved she has never hunted before. This can be a new experience for us both, to learn together. We make the short walk through the town centre, towards the library. I avert my eyes from the spots where I moved the dead people weeks earlier, where I watched the soldier shoot the mugger.

I don't mention to Maggie I was there on the day of the riot. It's not something I want to relive by talking about it, so I let her talk to me about root ginger, and all the wonderful things it is useful for. Before I know it, we have walked down the steep hill and reached the library, which is built halfway between the top and bottom of the hill. The brief excitement I felt disappears quickly, as we look at the blackened ash door and window frames. We hadn't realised it, but the library had been set on fire at some point. The remains of all its knowledge are gone forever.

'There's other libraries,' Maggie says cheerfully, noticing my disappointment. 'In fact, we will take a car into the city, and find one.'

I shake my head, worried about the attention driving a car could cause. I remember footage of people being pulled from cars in the riots. It was terrifying. We don't know what the city is like, how many survived. I am just about to protest and open my mouth when the words run dry. Not too far in the distance is a hum of something loud that distracts me.

'Can you hear that, Maggie?'

She listens and nods. 'It sounds like motorbikes.'

The vibration is getting closer quickly, and my fight-or-flight response kicks in alongside my racing heart and I start to panic. I haven't seen anyone other than Maggie for two months.

'Who do you think it is? Should we hide?'

She takes a moment to think as the screeching gets louder.

'Take cover over there, behind that wall.'

There's a row of terraced houses over the road, with a car parked in front of a four-foot garden wall. I sprint over the cracks and weeds in the street, diving through the garden gate, squatting low, with my head poking over the brick. Maggie raises her gun to greet the oncoming vehicles. The first bike that materialises over the top of the hill is a red dirt bike. Its rider is instantly startled by Maggie and the gun. In his, panic the driver pulls on the brakes too hard and is catapulted over the handlebars, throwing him off before the bike crashes into a nearby tree. He has a helmet on, and we see him move. Thank God, we didn't kill him! Maggie signals me to stay where I am as we hear the sound of more bikes approaching. The motorcyclist forces himself to sit up, dazed. There's a large backpack weighing him down. He removes his helmet and I see a trickle of blood on his head. He's young. Maybe even younger than me.

'Are you okay?' Maggie shouts over.

He nods, touching his injury, and then realises the other bikes are almost upon us. His expression changes to fear and he screams.

'Run!'

Forcing himself to scramble to his feet, he starts off sprinting down the hill like a drunk, as a quad bike with two riders appears on the brow. They have balaclavas on and are dressed in black. They spot him running, quick on his trail, ignoring Maggie as they pass her in a blur, catching up to the young lad. The passenger of the quad swings a cricket bat and knocks him back to the floor, as the driver brings them to a screeching halt. They jump off, and sickeningly start to beat him with the bat, over and over again.

'STOP IT!' I scream, jumping up from behind the wall. I am loud enough to make them pause and I watch in horror as a handgun is raised at me. A short *pop* echoes through the air as the trigger is pulled. The bullet hits the window of the parked car before me, shattering glass.

'Shit!'

I duck back down and hear the resounding echoing *bang* from the shotgun. Maggie has fired. A quick succession of *pop, pop, pop* is returned. Then silence. I have no idea what's happening. I decide to crawl to a different part of the garden, sharp stones pressing into my knees and palms. I raise my head above the wall just as the quad bike's engine restarts. I duck down again, feeling trapped. The noise comes closer to where I am, and I hear a menacing voice loudly shout as it slows.

'We'll be back to find, and fucking kill you bitches!' Another round of gunfire and more smashing glass cascades nearby. They speed away to a return of Maggie's booming gunshots, reverberating through the street.

She screams after them. 'Come and fucking try!'

The noise reduces to the distant hum once again and I stand, my eyes searching for Maggie. She is safe, panting, kneeling behind another parked car by the library. I run over.

'Maggie. Are you hurt?'

She grins. 'No. I'm fine. I'm fine.'

But she's shaking. I help her up and check her over, just in case.

'Who were they? Did you see their jackets?' I refer to the upside down cross.

'I'll find out, but we're not safe right now, we have to go.'

'What about the boy?'

We both turn to look down the street, where a river of blood runs towards a nearby grate. His body lies still. The bag he had is gone, and there's a tin of something near his head.

'I don't think we can help him,' Maggie says. 'It's best you don't look.'

I think about the community centre. I think about moving my own parents' bodies. I am stronger than Maggie gives me credit for, and I must know if he is dead.

I take a deep breath and walk slowly towards him. I see the tin, now. A cheap brand of spaghetti hoops. His face has been beaten so badly, you cannot make out where the eyes and nose once were. It is a mashed pulp of blood and flesh.

He is dead. Killed for a few cans of food.

'We need to move his body,' I shout back.

'Tomorrow, Elle. If it's safe.'

I nod, pick up the spaghetti, and we make our way back home.

That evening I spend at Maggie's. She insists. She is afraid and needs the company, but I suspect she is wanting to protect *me*. I don't protest. We are both shaken to learn there is some kind of gang that is hunting people for food and can only imagine they came from the city. There was no hesitation in killing that boy. Pure, brutal murder.

'Survival of the fittest,' Maggie sighs.

We sit the night out in darkness, too worried to light a candle in case they come back to roam the streets looking for us.

Present day - The Hive, Part One

Tom returns to the room with a hamper. An actual picnic hamper made from woven wicker. Inside are three fully cooked wood pigeons with their heads still intact. A couple of small handmade burnt bread rolls, and raw carrots. He also has a glass bottle with murky liquid sloshing inside, and a packet of baby wipes. Nothing else.

'Seriously?' Sarah seethes, taking the bottle from Tom's hand.

'I'm tired, Sarah, I don't want to argue, and sorry, Elle. There's nothing for her here. Apparently one of the slave girls is pregnant, to his second-in-command, but they haven't done anything about it yet. So, no supplies.'

Tom says the sentence so casually, I almost don't take in the words properly. But then I do, and they rain down on me like acid.

'Slave girls?' I spit venomously. He holds up his hands in defence.

'I didn't say I was okay with it. I'm not okay with it, but this is what they do. I can't do anything about it.'

'Isn't he *your cousin?*'

Red patches spring up on his neck and cheeks, and he whispers in a stressed frenzy, trying not to raise his voice:

'You saw him, right? You saw how dangerous he is? The only reason we're not all dead right now is because he's my fucking cousin! Christ, I'm sorry. I didn't mean to take this out on you Elle, it's not your fault.'

There's no sense in continuing to argue. It doesn't solve my problem in settling Emma. Instead, I take the wipes and get about cleaning her, leaving her half naked to run around whilst we eat the measly offerings of food. At some point Kasper donates his jacket to cover her and keep her warm, and I lie down with her after a while, stroking her hair as she yawns and snuggles into me. Feeling uncontrollable tiredness pull me into harrowing dreams.

'Hey.' Tom's smooth voice wakes me.

I'm not sure how long I've been asleep, but the candles have all been doused except one, and the noise of sleeping bodies vibrates throughout the room.

'You were having a nightmare,' he whispers, sitting himself down next to me. I feel groggy and dry mouthed.

'Sorry,' I mumble.

'No, it's okay. I am just worried about you.'

I sit up, and glance at Emma next to me, who remains in perfect slumber.

'Don't suppose you want any moonshine?'

'Moonshine?'

The word is alien to me, and Tom smirks as he passes me the wine bottle. 'It's good stuff, have a taste.'

I unscrew the cap and take a sniff. It's like pure ethanol and it makes me cough, much to Tom's amusement.

'No, thanks!' I say, handing back the bottle. 'What time is it?'

'No idea, early morning?'

'Huh, you can't sleep?' I ask.

'Not here. Not when the safety of all of you is my responsibility. As soon as it gets light, we're leaving. Get you and Emma to The Hive, where it's safe.'

I nod, feeling guarded, but also softened, and we sit quietly for a minute or two. I rub my eyes thinking about the dreams that came: a mixture of Maggie screaming, with motorbikes on a wet street, leaving trails of blood behind them. My mum and dad sitting on the grassy knoll in town, and then *Bang*. Gunshots. I'm trying to reach them all, but I can't get near. My legs are like lead.

I feel a spike of adrenaline, as haunting images of Maggie flash in my mind.

'Can I ask you a question?'

'Sure.'

'How did you know that's what Maggie wanted. You know, to end her life like that? Why didn't she tell *me?*'

'How old are you, Elle?'

I'm taken aback by the question. Not sure how it's relevant to anything.

'I'm nineteen, almost twenty. Why? How old are you?'

His grin is distorted in the dancing shadows that move across his face. Amused by my defensive retort.

'Well, I'm twenty-eight, almost twenty-nine, but my point being, you might not feel it, but you're so young, Elle.'

I open my mouth to protest, but he raises a hand. 'Hear me out, you're so young and you've had to bear so much. Maggie knew this. She never pitied you, but it hurt her deeply that you spent your eighteenth year dealing with this shit show, dealing with losing all your friends, family, and way of life.'

I contemplate his words. Listening.

'Maggie told me she always had wanted children. Nature had never allowed it. She told me you were the closest thing to a daughter she had ever experienced, and in this short space of time, she grew to love you. You made her live longer, she wanted to go on and survive, for you.'

Tears spring immediately, and I wipe them away as he continues.

'When I met Maggie, you were the first thing she spoke about. She was so proud of you. She didn't want your last memories of her to be someone who was weak and wasting away, and she didn't want you to have to live alone after she had gone. She was desperate for you to be safe. She literally begged me to come and find you and take you with us if something happened. She said she would always be at the trade meets, and if ever she wasn't, we had to come and find out why. Keep you and Emma safe. She said when she got too weak, she would kill herself before the cancer did.'

I exhale a deep trembling breath, trying hard not to sob and wake the sleeping.

'I have been so afraid, Tom. I was afraid of you. Even when Maggie told me I could trust you. I did not want to trust you. Maggie kept me safe; she kept me alive.'

'I understand,' he says diplomatically. 'But you kept each other alive,' he corrects. 'I'm sorry you've lost her, and you *can* trust us. You can trust me.'

I wipe my nose and eyes again, wanting to believe him, and I turn to look at him, really look at him. He has kind eyes I decide, as we stare at each other, and I nod, making him simper shyly.

Streaks of pink light eventually begin to reach through the window, and the others begin to stir in the dawn light.

'I need the loo,' Sarah announces, yawning and stretching from her spot on the floor. I've been bursting for a while but afraid to leave the sanctuary this room provides. I'm sure Boy will be glad of the opportunity to get outside, too.

'Can I come with you?'
She nods.

'I'll watch Emma,' Aisha offers.
I smile and follow Sarah to the door. I feel like I can trust Aisha. Emma seems to like her. I wonder if she reminds Emma of her mother, with her dark skin and hair.

'Wait,' Ant shouts over to Sarah before we leave. 'Take this.'
He holds out his large knife, which she stuffs into the back of her jeans. This doesn't feel like a normal trip to the bathroom. We tiptoe down the narrow passageway, with Boy skipping beside me. I try to keep up. She has woken up agitated and storms darkly down the hall, with me following tentatively

behind. I take the opportunity to speak to her, now we are alone.

'I'm assuming you're not okay being here?' I whisper.
I see her bristle. She stops walking and turns to me.

'It's not safe here. I don't trust Christopher or this alliance. Christopher is a hyena. You know about hyenas?'
Her eyes are wild with her rhetorical question.

'They are terrifying. They skulk in the shadows, waiting like sadistic cowards. Dirty, vicious, and ruthless. Their strength comes from their numbers, stealing treasures that aren't theirs from others. They watch the skies for circling vultures. Waiting. You can never trust a hyena, even when it looks like it is smiling at you.'
I see her eyes are filled with tears again, but she blinks them back.

'Tom is a fool to trust him.'
She turns again and sets off at a furious pace. I don't know what to say, but I understand her sentiment. We make our way through the maze of rooms, trying to avoid the sleeping quarters, until we finally see a door that opens towards the back of the building. It's a fire exit. Unlocked. We step out into a misty morning, full of birdsong, where morning dew sits upon every surface. I spot the water tank and four

Portaloos nearby. Boy gets the scent of something immediately and runs off. I let him. There's nobody around, so we go about our business quietly. The loo is cleaner than I expected, it's obviously regularly maintained, but I'm quick to use it, and am happy to step back outside afterwards. I take a short stroll waiting for Sarah, looking for Boy. Not wanting to shout, I walk over to look at the large plastic water tank. It stands at least ten feet tall, with a simple tap at the bottom, and I make a mental note to fill up some water bottles for Emma before we leave today. When I turn back around, I jump out of my skin to find I'm almost face-to-face with Christopher, who is walking straight towards me. He's not alone. There's a thin, mousy haired, broken-looking woman by his side. She's barefooted, carrying a large box full of empty water bottles, and I notice bruises on her face.

'Well, the early bird catches the red-headed worm,' he chuckles, looking me up and down crudely.

'You, you're new to Tom's family of little whelps. What's your name?'

He steps aside so the woman can access the tank. She doesn't look at me. Just drops to her knees silently and begins filling up the bottles at the tap. My throat has gone pathetically dry, and I look behind him, back to the toilet boxes, searching for Sarah, but she's not there.

'Name?' he demands with a threatening smile, as he takes a cigarette and lighter from his pocket.

'E-Elle,' I stutter, starting to panic.

Sarah's words echo in my mind *'You can never trust a hyena, even when it looks like it is smiling at you.'*

I take a step away, glancing at the kneeling woman. He notices my subtle move and shakes his head.

'You don't leave until I tell you that you can, and don't look at her. Saffron is not in my favour right now. Isn't that right, Saffy?'

The woman doesn't answer.

'I have to get back,' I croak, and I try to take a step past him. He grabs my arm roughly, smiling again, the lit cigarette in his mouth brushing my cheek. My heart threatens to explode as I desperately try to shake him off me.

'I will repeat in case you didn't hear me the first time. You don't leave until I tell you that you can.'

Feeling his grip on my body, I look directly into his eyes: they're as cold as ice, which sends a shiver down my spine, but infuriates me at the same time. This man, this monster, is responsible for the months I've spent terrified of the sound of engines ripping up my town. This animal has orchestrated the deaths of God knows how many people to satisfy the insatiable hunger of his followers. He preys on the vulnerable, destroys the weak. He's the most dangerous person I have ever known, and yet here I am, suddenly switching from fear to fury, staring him down with anger and defiance.

'Chris, let her go!'

Relief washes over me as Tom, Ant, and Sarah jog towards us. Sarah must have raised the others, but Christopher doesn't flinch. He keeps smiling at me, staring with those frosty eyes whilst squeezing my arm tighter.

'How much for her, Tom?' he shouts, and for a second my heart leaps into my throat in sickening anticipation.

'She's not for sale, Chris.' Tom's tone is cautious, but there's an edge to it, like a threat.

'Christ, Tom, it's the apocalypse. Everything's for sale.'

'Let go of me, you sadistic fuck!' I spit.

His smile turns nasty, the amused gleam in his eyes suddenly dark. I have never seen someone's face change so quick.

'This bitch for fucking real, Tom?'

I glare at him as the tension builds between us, and even though I don't look at Tom, I feel him pleading with me to back down. Even the poor woman on her knees has stopped filling up the water bottles, as we continue to stare each other out. Then Boy appears. He is running through the foliage towards us, barking and growling when he sees the hold Christopher has on me.

'Good boy,' I whisper through gritted teeth, never averting my gaze.

There's a brief pause, where even I don't know the outcome of the next few seconds, but he releases me. I take a step backwards, refusing to break eye contact first, as he takes a drag on the cigarette.

'Interesting company you keep, Tom.'

From the corner of my eye, I see Sarah frantically waving at me to join them, and I call Boy over, who immediately stops his audio attack on Christopher. Finally, I turn away, and rejoin my new companions. Tom gives me a quick half-smile as I pass him, making sure we get back inside, whilst Sarah puts her arms around me and guides me away.

'Jesus, Elle.' She exhales as we re-enter the building. I'm physically shaking, adrenaline pumping, and all I want to do is see Emma and leave this place. It's ironic, but I can't wait to get to The Hive.

I don't know what Tom and Christopher spoke about after we left, but Tom storms in looking flushed and tells us all to pack up and leave, right now. There's no hesitation. Sarah tells Aisha very elaborately about my standoff, and I seem to have gained some kind of hero status in her eyes. I can't enjoy my moment, though, not when I think about the woman, Saffron. That we are just going to leave her here and do nothing about it. I wrap Kasper's jacket back around Emma and carry her close to me as we make our way back through the house. The atmosphere is hostile.

Our horse with empty cart, and Ant and Sarah's horse are waiting for us at the front of the house, along with an alarming leaving party. Christopher is there, with two men at each side of him, wearing balaclavas, holding assault rifles. The big, bearded man is there too, and I feel angry eyes boring into us.

'These are all his commanders,' Sarah whispers.
I hop onto the back of the cart with Kasper, noticing a slight movement from one of the henchmen. He steps forward and whispers something to Christopher and I feel like he's looking directly at me. Christopher's face remains unchanged as he says something back. I squeeze Emma even tighter, feeling a lump of fear in the pit of my stomach as I realise Kasper,

Emma and I are completely exposed and vulnerable in the back of this wagon.

Christopher shouts over. 'When you return, be sure to bring Justin, Tom. Like I said: no more chances.'

There's a stark silence before our party starts to move away slowly. This is when I notice Boy. He is still sniffing around at the front of the house; unaware we are leaving.

'BOY!' I yell. 'COME HERE, BOY!'

I see an unpleasant smile cross Christopher's face. He says something back to his aide as Boy hears my call and comes running. We are still only about fifty metres away from them, and in a horrifying moment I see the man raise his rifle. I turn away, quickly shielding Emma, and scream, expecting the gunfire that rings out to hit us. BANG. My ears ring, Emma screams, and Ant's horse rears up onto its hind quarters, nearly throwing them off. There's an ugly, shrill sound which pierces through the air at the same time. A chilling yelp.

Boy is cut down with one shot.

Tom stops the horse and cart, turning around in his seat, wide-eyed.

'What the fuck!' he cries.

I am howling, looking at Boy's unmoving body as blood pools around him on the gravel lane.

'YOU FUCKING ANIMAL!' I scream, and then I cry into Emma's hair.

Kasper shuffles over to hold me tightly, and I feel him trembling as he turns his head. 'Go, Tom. Now!'

With panic, Tom cracks the whip and we set off quickly towards the open gates, holding on tightly as the wheels hit the bumps and the rocks with speed, throwing us around. I wipe my eyes and look back at the monsters laughing on the porch of the stately home, whilst Boy lays dead before them.

Then, for a moment, time just freezes.

I squint, almost unable to understand what I am seeing.

Is this real? This can't be real. *He* can't be real. But he is. Handing Emma to Kasper, I half stand, and I feel as though I am in some kind of cruel dream, being ripped in half as I stare. I hear my throat release a harrowing whimper.

The man who shot Boy has removed his balaclava.

He turns to meet my gaze with a fierce expression I barely recognise, but as his dark curls lift off his face in the breeze, our eyes lock. I am staring horrified at the man I used to love.

Danny.

He's alive, and he is here.

Christopher's right-hand man. A leader of The Chosen.

Present day - The Hive, Part Two

Butterflies and bees swarm across the meadows as we pass, and long grass creeps up from every corner of the once-smooth tarmacked roads, reaching up through the cracks to the warm sun that beats down. We pass through ghost towns filled with a new level of nature. The chorus of birdsong so loud amongst the silence of mankind. Deer, rabbits, and wild horses scattering before us.

But at this moment, I cannot fully appreciate the beauty of this new world. Knowing Danny is alive, that he is one of *them*, a monster. It has broken something deep inside me. I have not told the others; I can't bring myself to speak his name.

After, we travelled far enough away from The Chosen to feel safe. Tom stopped the cart and let me sob unashamedly into his comforting embrace whilst he begged forgiveness for bringing us all there. I cried harder than I had done for Maggie, and had a moment where I wondered what I looked like to them, falling apart over the death of a dog when we had all lost people, but I couldn't tell them. I couldn't breathe the words that I saw Danny, that I loved him once, that I had wished him alive so many, many times. So, I let everyone think I was having some kind of PTSD breakdown, and graciously, they let me.

Christopher left us nothing for our return journey. Only the half-filled water bottles Aisha managed to scrape together before we hastily left, and some stale biscuits found in one of the houses en-route. During the last few miles, hunger, thirst, and tiredness creep over us all; it has been a hard, hard day, for us all.

I have been sitting for most of the journey in numb silence, passively watching the world through glazed-over eyes. I am tired and haven't been paying much attention—until we start to track up the slip road of a motorway I recognise. When I was little, about ten years old, I was obsessed with dancing. Dad used to ferry me this exact way to a dance studio at another city via the motorway every Tuesday night. This went on for about two years, until I outgrew the hobby. I remember the journey, and this stretch, well. However, the motorway is now desolate except for the odd abandoned lorry or burned-out army surplus truck rusting in its skeleton frame, surrounded by weeds, cracks and potholes, but the view is the same. As we cross, I can see the river glistening below in the afternoon sun, the way it used to do in the summer every Tuesday. There's a heron, and swans on the water. A little village in the distance, like a picture-postcard. It makes me smile.

'The Hive!' Tom yells from his driving seat.

I look to where he points further afield and see farm fields that span for miles between the river and the railway tracks, a vast woodland along the boundary. It's not flat ground; one of the fields cultivates to a gradual summit, and on it, there's a mass of caravans, tents, and a real bustle of life.

It feels surreal.

Our little entourage exits the next slip road, where a roadblock was put in place at some point, but the concrete boulders have all been smashed to make an exit. We continue through it and along a main road, until we reach a left turn onto a farm track. Hung over the post of an open metal gate, there's a wooden sign with letters carved deeply into it: THE HIVE.

We follow the trail for about half a mile amongst a dense bluebell woodland, and I hear the river in the distance. Eventually, the path opens wider to a large farmyard.

'I basically grew up here,' Tom says proudly.

The remains of three big sheds sit eerily quiet as we pass; a fire has destroyed them, including what was once a large house. The upstairs rooms are exposed, and charred bricks lie scattered across the floor. Someone has wrapped tape around the house and has hand-scrawled signs warning others to keep away from the danger. I wonder if it was Tom who did that.

We pass through the yard and reach another gate. This one is attached to tall heras fencing that stretches all the way to the river one way, and right across the perimeter the other way. Behind the fence the woodland has ended, and I see wide open fields with a warren of animal pens close to the meandering river. The land inclines slightly onto meadows of cows, and sheep, and a silo on top of a hill, next to the caravans and tents I saw from the motorway. I peer around Aisha's head in wonder. There's every kind of animal here: pigs, donkeys, goats, and I'm sure I see an ostrich and a zebra.

Chickens and ducks run around freely, and there's a large vegetable patch, big enough to rival Maggie's allotment. The Hive is exactly as its name suggests: busy with people doing all kinds of chores.

'Heard you before I saw you,' says a stocky, ginger-haired man with a big grin. He is unlocking the gate for us, and I immediately notice the rifle strapped across his back.

'Thomas!' says Tom affectionately, with a return smile.

'All quiet on the western front?'

'All quiet, gaffer.'

'That might change,' Tom says, bringing the cart to a stop.

'Radio for a buddy and get them gunned up.'

'Oh?' questions Thomas, pushing the gate open.

'I'll debrief The Hive tomorrow, just don't let Justin be on guard duty.'

Ant and Sarah bring their horse around to the side of our cart.

'We're exhausted, going to the stables, Tom. I'll find Justin and have that chat.'

Tom nods and they canter away towards the railway bridge, where I notice more horses and some stables. Kasper shuffles over, jumping off from the cart.

'I stay. With Thomas.'

'Good man, Kasper. I'll find someone to relieve you soon and bring some food.'

Kasper nods, helping to shut and lock the gate again, and we set off slowly towards the hill, the horse clearly tired now. Emma is stirring, waking from a brief nap and is agitated.

'Good timing, sweetheart,' I say, kissing her forehead and pointing at the animals. 'We're here. Look.'

It's been a hard few days, and I'm hoping we can try to get some kind of peace soon, but I am nervous with anticipation of this new life and these strangers, lots of strangers. I am happy to see a few children running around, as Tom said there would be, and for a while I'm distracted from my tortured thoughts of Danny.

The horse brings us up to the silo and my eyes track around my new surroundings. Washing lines full of clothes, bikes and toys left in the compacted mud under a few sparse trees. Theres a variation of caravans ranging from big to small, with fairy lights, and bunting decorated between them. My eyes follow a path down to the riverbank, where I see an odd-looking, curved brick building. It's small, with a hand-dug trench wrapping around it like a moat; I can't figure out what it is.

We stop, directly in the shadow of the silo, and I see there's quite a crowd walking up towards us. Aisha jumps off our wagon and comes straight round to take Emma from me. Her kind eyes apologetic about the interest our arrival has caused. I scramble off the back, sore and tired from the journey, and try to smile at the curious faces, but fail to hold my gaze for long enough to look sincere at the group of women, men, and children staring at me. I am thankful when Tom jumps down with a smile, distracting them with his charm. Shielding me.

'Our journey has been extremely difficult. As you can imagine.'

An older-looking man shuffles directly towards Tom. He is bald, with a white beard, and he points at the cart.

'It's empty, did we not receive tradeables?'

'I'm going to update everyone tomorrow, Alistair. Please, all is well.'

'No sugar for your tea again, Heidi.' A round, friendly-faced woman chuckles to her friend as they turn back around and herd away the children that stand gaping.

'Who is that?' I hear the curious voice of the smallest. A little boy no older than about four or five, pointing at me.

'Tom will tell us tomorrow,' Heidi replies, turning back to me with a kind smile.

Aisha returns Emma, who has started squirming and moaning, just as Kasper's jacket falls to the floor in a sodden heap. She picks it up.

'I'll sort this. Will you be joining us for dinner?'

I feel so overwhelmed I can't string a reply together. Again, Tom comes to my rescue.

'Let her sit this one out. I'd say you'd be happy for some quiet time? I can bring something over later, after I've shown you to your new home?'

I nod.

'Thanks,' I whisper quietly.

I watch as he unstraps the cart from the horse, and gently guides it to a trough beneath the silo. We are alone. I look at the empty cart, never having realised the sacrifice he must have made to keep us safe, and I think it's time for me to put my pride aside.

'Thank you, for protecting me. Back with Christopher. I'm sorry if that has cost you, The Hive, greatly.'

'I was naive to think the trip to The Chosen would be anything more than difficult; you have nothing to apologise or thank me for, Elle.'

Toms voice is strained. As he fusses over the horse, I breathe in the farm smell, turning around to face the river and the setting sunlight that beams across the lush fields.

'What's that building?' I ask, pointing at the brick structure by the water.

'Our oat mill,' Tom replies proudly. 'Justin built us it.'

Justin, there's that name again.

'Is this why Christopher wants him? To build him a mill?'

'Something like that. Justin is an exceptional human being, but you'll find out everything there is to know, eventually. Let me show you to your humble abode.'

For the first time today, his mischievous grin is back as he leads me to where a dozen or more caravans sit, in all shapes and sizes. There are a few trees around, and past them is a large white gazebo, like a circus tent but without the sides. A big cooking pit sits to the right of it, and a couple of people are huddled around, prodding, and poking at several plucked pheasants hanging from a metal crossbar.

There seems to be what looks like a small wooden stage inside the tent, and lots of little light bulbs crisscrossing around; it must look pretty at night. There's a mismatch of tables and chairs, and I see a guitar propped up by an empty stool. I don't notice Tom's delight at the wonder in my face, but I hear it in his voice.

'Impressive, isn't it? We all eat there, every night. We have music, good food, and sometimes, if we dare try it, homemade ale, cider, or wine.'

There are no words for how I feel. All this time, alone. Scavenging, scared, barely surviving. This was here, all this time.

'Do the lights work?' I ask rather stupidly, expecting a burst of laughter, but he replies very seriously.

'Justin creates solar-powered batteries. We have light, yes, and each caravan has some electric, sometimes. It works okay for the basics like toasters and kettles.'

'Toasters? Kettles?' I repeat.

'Yes,' He laughs 'I'll bring some to you if there's none already inside. Here we are.'

We stop outside a small, mouldy-looking caravan. Its once white paint is peeling, and the tyres are both flat, but it's held up by wooden stops and looks sturdy. I notice the solar panel on the roof immediately.

'This is one of the better empty ones unfortunately, but it's only temporary, we are wanting to move people back into the village houses, but for now, it's better than nothing. Justin is hoping to build a hydro dam and wind turbine too, which could power the houses, but the logistics behind it are a bit beyond our reach right now.'

'So, the caravan has power?'

'Yes!' He laughs. 'There should be a key in the door, make yourself at home and I'll gather some supplies for you and Emma.'

He blows a raspberry to make her laugh, screwing up his face before he leaves.

'I'll make sure someone is round later with supplies.'

I feel like I've walked into some bizarre upside world as I step into the caravan. I put Emma down to explore, and I rush over to the toaster and kettle in the tiny kitchen area, pressing down their buttons like a child. They work.

'Oh my God!' I shriek. 'Emma, look! We have electricity!' Emma pays me no attention whatsoever; she has found a cushion with an embroidered picture of a brown dog, and is patting it gently, like she used to do to Boy, babbling in her own baby language. There's a small electric radiator next to her, beside a little coffee table.

'No way!' I yell, and bound over to it, press the switch, and hey presto, on comes the radiator, an orange glow lighting up the room. Emma is mesmerised.

I suddenly don't care that the caravan smells musty, that it's small, or has weird brown-and-yellow decor. We have heat, and lights. I'm so overwhelmed I feel tears spring into my eyes, and if that wasn't enough, there's a knock at the door ten minutes later. When I open it, there's nobody there, only a pushchair filled with carrier bags full of things. I stand mute looking at it all. Clothes for Emma, cloth nappies, soap, bottles of water. There's everything I need; it's like Christmas when I haul it all inside. The last bag is the best. It has a curved, golden loaf of fresh bread; I haven't eaten or even seen bread in over a year. I sniff it. It's so good. There's also a small glass jar of homemade jam. I almost fall over myself, scrambling for a knife in one of the kitchen drawers, trying to slice it and get it in the toaster quickly. I pull off untoasted pieces and give some to Emma, who gives me a big smile as she greedily stuffs it into her mouth, saliva dripping from her chin. A tear rolls down my face.

'I think we're going to be okay here, Em.'

Present - The Hive, Part Three

Emma and I wake up snuggling together in the small double bed of the caravan. We've slept like logs. The sun is already shining through the thin curtain, and the little run-down tin can is heating up nicely; not that we needed any more heat, the electric radiator kept us warm all night. I kiss Emma's hair and sit up, stretching and listening to voices.

There's laughter, a clunk of glass bottles, and some pleasantries being thrown around outside. I peer through a slit in the curtains and feel an anxious knot in the pit of my stomach. Being thrust so suddenly into a community is nerve-wracking, and I think I'll be expected to meet some of these people today, but Maggie's voice is in my mind.

'This is the way forward, Elle.'

Of course, I know now that she was right all along.

Keeping my mind busy, I change Emma, dressing her with the donated clothes from the bags, and pop some more bread in the toaster, putting water in the kettle for a black coffee.

There's a knock at the door.

Right, breathe, I tell myself, tentatively opening it. Tom stands grinning, holding a full glass bottle of what look likes milk. He's clean, all the sweat and dirt from our travelling washed off his skin and hair, and he is wearing clean clothes: jeans and a tight, blue cotton T-shirt. I avert my eyes bashfully as I notice large bulging biceps for the first time. He nervously runs his hands through his blond hair.

'Did you sleep well?'

I'm aware I probably look a dishevelled mess, still wearing the same clothes from before Maggie's, and I subconsciously try to flatten my knotty hair with my fingers.

'Oh, yeah. We did, thanks. Like babies.'

He smiles. 'That's great. Here, I've brought you some milk, fresh from one of our cows. I wondered if you'd let me show you around today. Show you where to get food and water, and where to have a warm shower.'

I clutch my fingers around the milk bottle. The bottle's not cold, but it's definitely real milk, and did I hear him right? *Warm shower?* I am stunned into silence, and I just nod as though I am simple, as the toaster pops. He grins again.

'Okay, well, great. I'll be with Justin at the water mill.'

He points towards the river, making sure I know where I'm going.

'Thanks,' I mumble. 'I'll find you.'

I shut the door, my rapid pulse inconveniently causing my pale skin to blush, and I think my cheeks must match the colour of my hair.

'Christ,' I say out loud. I do not need a crush on Tom in my life right now.

I feed Emma and pour a bit of the milk into a cup I find in a cupboard. She likes it and has a white moustache of residue across her top lip which makes me laugh. It's a little sour-tasting for my liking, but I'm sure I will get used to it.

I'm aware I have nothing else to wear, and I sniff my armpits, pulling a face. The best I can do is a quick rinse in the sink with some of the bottled water and soap given to us. The sound of a warm shower is heaven. I strap Emma in the pushchair that appeared last night and feel like we are off on an outing. Navigating out of the caravan, I lock it and pocket the key. The springtime air is fresh as it hits our skin, with sun rays creeping through the clouds. There's a smell on the breeze, too: cow dung, or something similar, and animal noises encompass the surroundings: chickens cluck, dogs bark, and there are *baas* and *moos* in the distance. A real-life, working farm. There's also a bustle of life from the inhabitants, as I look down towards the gates and fields we came through yesterday. Men and women come and go with purpose. Smoke billows from somewhere; shouts, laughter, and commands filter around. It doesn't feel real, any of it, and thoughts of Danny are now pushed way back in my mind.

I walk us down to the funny little brick building, where I can see Tom talking animatedly to a taller, mousy-haired man in dark overalls. I assume this is the elusive Justin that Christopher is so interested in. They are pointing at the little trench that winds from the river and around the mill. Tom throws his right hand in the air, making a spinning movement with his finger, and Justin nods in agreement. I feel like I am intruding, the closer I get, and that it is best to turn around and wait until Tom looks less busy, but I am spotted and called over before I get the chance.

'Elle!' He does not hide the delight in his voice when he spots me, and I fight to hide the heat in my face, throwing a reserved smile at Tom, and Justin.

'Great, you made it. This is Elle and baby Emma, who I told you about.'

Justin wipes his hands on his trouser leg and smiles warmly. He is in his forties, I am guessing, with thick, dark-rimmed spectacles and a prominent side parting. He looks intelligent, but also athletic at the same time.

'Justin, pleased to meet you. Elle. Is that short for Eleanor?'

He holds out his hand for me to shake; the action feels so alien.

'No, it's Elizabeth.'

'That's funny,' he says. 'I had a daughter called Elizabeth, but her nickname was Beth. She was quite a bit younger than you, though, but adamant she had decided to change it permanently, much to our disproval. I bet your parents didn't like *Elle* either, did they?'

I look up and smile sympathetically. 'Dad hated *Elle*.'

'Knew it!' He beams.

'Justin is the Einstein of the new world,' Tom explains. 'We have a few issues with the flour mill here.'

'Nothing that can't be fixed.' Justin smirks. 'I'll let you know if I need anything, Tom, you have more important things to attend to, like showing these young ladies around.' Right on cue, Emma lets free a loud babble in her own language, and we all laugh.

'Okay, I guess that's told us, then. Shall we?' Tom leads the way, and walks in step with me, proudly showing me the sights of The Hive.

I learn the farm was Tom's grandparents' before the virus. He spent a large chunk of his life here, helping around the farm; and most of the animals, barring the ostrich and the zebra, which were fetched by one of the settlers, are originally from here.

There are eight fields in total, which include the one near the entrance gate, split into four or five smaller pens for the donkeys, goats, zebra, ostrich and five pigs. He has nine cows and two bullocks. Three of the cows are expecting calves any day now. There are twenty-five sheep, and six horses. There's a large field of wheat, ready to be harvested in a few months, and he explains how they worked hard through the winter to clear a smaller field for planting root vegetables.

Tom is so patient with me as I ask a million questions about how they sustain themselves. He puts the bulk of their survival on the shoulders of his grandparents, always making sure the silo was full of seed, and having a tank full of red diesel for the combine harvester and the tractors. It helped them get through a difficult winter as more and more survivors arrived here, and of course he also extends his gratitude to Justin. Major General Justin Sanderson, in fact. A man who worked directly for biotech and renewable energy departments in the MOD, starting his professional life as a hydrogen energy system engineer, there seems to be nothing he can't do. He is the creator of The Hive's solar panels, and the water purification system installed both here and at The

Chosen. He has created the flour mill, a heated water contraption, and is showing others how to make composting toilets. Tom says he is even looking at creating a kind of plumbing system, all while I was scratching in the darkness of my freezing cold home because I'd run out of firewood.

Justin is passionate that The Hive, and the other survivors of the world will not make the same mistakes as our generation did. That we will learn how to live with nature, how to be considerate to our environment, how to earn our place again in the world. So the earth will never again see us as a threat to her soil and try to wipe us out.

I am awestruck at this.

It is no wonder Christopher craves Justin's knowledge, and after only one short conversation, I can see why someone like Justin, would detest someone like Christopher.

We walk and talk most of the day. We take Emma to see the small animals, and I meet Jennifer, the same kind-looking woman who came to greet the cart with the children yesterday. It turns out she is the one who brought me the pushchair and the baby supplies. She looks after the orphans here. A former childminder. She promises that she will find more things for us and drop them around when she can, and I can tell she already adores Emma. They spend a good hour together laughing at the noises the pigs make.

I find out that everybody, each of the sixty-two people that reside here, has a job, whether that is chopping firewood; hunting deer, pheasant, or rabbit for the communal dinners; cooking, or tending to the vegetables and crops; fishing; washing clothes; scavenging for supplies; fixing fences; or even looking after the animals.

It seems the list is endless.

When the afternoon begins to seep into evening, I am more accustomed to how The Hive operates. I know that the shower system is rostered, I know where to dispose of toilet waste. Food waste goes in a bucket for the animals, including bones. Clothes are recycled and mended. It's a working cog, and I'm feeling pretty excited about becoming part of it.

I sigh with guilt; Maggie *was* right. I wish I was able to tell her.

'Can I sit with you at dinner tonight?' Tom asks, walking us back to our caravan.

I realise I'm famished. The Hive eats twice a day here. Breakfast; usually porridge, or bread with jam or honey, and dinner. Communal dinner is always the pinnacle treat of the day where everyone gets involved. It will be something Emma and I will have to get used to.

'Yes, thank you.'

'Great, okay. I saw Ant and George come back with a few rabbits earlier, so it won't be long before things get going. Luke and Marina are our main chefs, they are like wizards in the kitchen. You'll love it.'

Tom practically beams, ruffling his hair and I smile at his enthusiasm.

'Could I just ask one more question, though, Tom, before you go? I'd like to try that shower if possible, and to freshen up. Would that be, okay? I just don't have any spare things, or anyone to watch Emma.'

'Yes, sure, no problem!' he spurts. 'I never even thought. I'll make some arrangements, hold tight.'

He skips off and I bring Emma into the caravan with a doll made from twigs and wrapped vine leaves that Jennifer gave us. I lie down on the cushions, feeling my heavy eyes shut. The same haunting sentiments running through my head.

Maggie would have loved it here.

I wake with a jolt ten minutes later to a knock at the door. My eyes instantly search, panicking, for Emma, but she's been good as gold and is playing quietly with the 'doll' which has been shredded into many pieces, most of it entering her mouth at some point. I remove the stick she is currently sucking on.

'Yak,' I say.

Opening the door, I'm pleased to see its Sarah. I smile warmly, encouraging her to come inside.

'I brought you a few spare things, me and Aisha guessed you're around our size, clothes-wise.'

She hands me a well-used carrier bag, full of clothes. I notice a bottle of something in there, a hairbrush, and a sharp tool. A razor!

'This is great, Sarah, thank you.'

She shrugs. 'Hey, look, it's no problem. I wanted to say, I'm sorry about the dog. I didn't get a chance to see you and talk properly afterwards. The trip to The Chosen, well, that was a lot for me. I just needed some space to, you know, process, and compose myself once we got home.'

'It's okay.' I say honestly, wanting to ask her more but deciding against it.

'Right, well. I can take Emma to Jennifer's if you like? She usually brings the kids to eat early, and they all go back to the big caravan, the one nearest to the woods. I know there's a cot there, and I think all the other kids are too big for it. Why don't you let your hair down, and let Jennifer look after

Emma tonight? There's a lot of people looking forward to meeting you.'

I bite my lip. I know the caravan she means, and I like Jennifer, but I feel nervous.

'I don't know, are you sure?'

She gives me one of her rare genuine smiles.

'*Yes*. Jennifer lives for kids, and you need a break, Elle; you've been through a hell of a lot, and you know what they say… it takes a village.'

She picks Emma up before I can protest, and walks to the door, turning around as she leaves.

'She's going to be just fine. Meet you at the 'à la carte' feast hall.' She winks and is gone.

I sit in unburdened silence for a moment, I don't remember what it feels like to not feel worried or stressed, and then I smile, and laugh like I haven't done in ages.

I feel like a silly teenager. Then I remember. I still am one: I'm not twenty for another couple of months so I'm going to make the most of it.

I rifle through the bag and pull out some lovely tops, a fleece, a dress, and some nice jeans. There's also fresh underwear and socks. The bottle contains shampoo, I think, and I'm so excited at the prospect of having a warm shower I almost forget the towel, which has been rolled tightly at the bottom of the bag for my use.

The shower isn't far away; they've built a plywood box around it, and there's a simple open/close sign that you can turn on the outside of the door. The water drains from a recycled water tank on the top of the box frame, and into a trench dugout all the way to the river. It's spectacular. I don't understand the actual mechanics of how it works, something to do with solar panels, and fibreglass insulation which warms the water.

I really think Justin must be a genius.

I waste no time in squeezing myself into the box room and locking the door. I strip off my clothes and put them in a plastic container by the door, along with my towel. Then the moment of truth. I turn on the shower. Beautiful warm water cascades down my back and over my hair. It's not hot enough to steam the place, but it's warm, and it's a shower.

I can barely believe it's been so long since I felt a luxury like this. I try to stick to the rules. No longer than six minutes per person, and one warm shower a week. This way, everyone should have a fair turn, and there should remain enough warm water to go around. Mine and Emma's assigned day is Tuesday, except for today, which is an exception. However, if

Tom hadn't told me today was Sunday I would have never known. Carefully, I shave hair from my body with the razor, another luxury I had almost forgotten about, and I wash my hair with the liquid Sarah gave me. I don't think I'm exaggerating when I say I feel like a different person when I leave that cubicle.

I put on the new clothes, and I think the white T-shirt fits me well. I towel-dry my hair the best I can, feeling my stomach groaning. It's time to go, dropping my used belongings back at the caravan before I do, but even though I'm physically ready. Mentally I'm a wreck.

My confidence begins to plummet the closer I get to the big white gazebo. It's full of residents of The Hive: some I saw briefly today; some I haven't met yet. There's talking, laughter and singing already, as a man sitting on a stool in the middle of the floor begins playing semi-familiar songs on the guitar, songs I think I recognise from the past.

Hundreds of solar lights twinkle from the canopy, and the smell of cooking permeates the air. I notice a queue of people lined up to collect their dinner.

Rabbit stew hot pot with dumplings, a chalkboard with white scrawled handwriting reads, and… *one roll of bread per person.*

I join the queue, looking at the floor whilst I wait, feeling insecure and nervous amongst so many people.

'Hey.'

I hear Tom's voice and look up. He's walking over to me, two empty bowls in hand. That grin on his face.

'Hey.' I smile.

'You'll need one of these,' he says, passing me the bowl and jumping the queue to stand with me. 'You look great! Enjoy the shower?'

'I think I'd forgotten what it is like to be clean!' I giggle.

'Don't get too used to it, us farm folk are usually covered in one thing or another.'

Our turn for stew and dumplings comes quickly, and Tom guides me to a free table, whilst the guitar player continues his renditions. We eat quickly, savouring the taste and devouring every drop and crumb.

'Good, isn't it.'

I nod, feeling a warm satisfying glow inside.

'Do you eat like this every day?'

'Pretty much, and so will you if you decide to stay.'

I stare at him, almost forgetting I had been determined to leave as soon as I could. It's only been a day and I'm already sure I do not belong anywhere else. A girl, a little bit younger than me, interrupts our table.

'Wine? Or water?' she asks.

Tom holds up two fingers, addressing her.

'Wine please, Rachael.'

Then, whispering back over to me, he says,

'Try this, it's blackberry wine; technically it shouldn't be ready to drink for another month, but it's quite edible.'

She hands us two ceramic mugs. Mine has a faded Father Christmas motif, and dark purple liquid sloshes around inside. I look at Tom to confirm it is indeed drinkable, but he's already gulping down the contents. I take a sip and instantly regret it, as a sharp, burning sourness courses down my throat, causing a coughing fit. Tom's laugh is louder than the music.

'Okay, half edible!' He chuckles at my screwed-up face.

'But you can't waste it.'

'If you say so.'

Trying not to breathe, I force the rest of the contents down, I gulp it until it's gone. He applauds.

'Impressive for your first moonshine.'

I flirt, already feeling lightheaded.

'How do you know that was my first?'

Now relaxed, we fall into easy conversation, barely noticing people collecting our dishes, or the change in beat and tempo to the music that's playing.

We talk about our lives before.

I find out he has a December birthday, and I listen to stories about him growing up on this farm since he was a boy. Driving tractors, ploughing fields, sheep-shearing, the lot. I tell him about my parents, college, and my friends: including who Emma is named after.

I miss out the part about Danny.

We drink more wine and move closer to the fire pit when the music stops and people start heading to their caravan homes. Sarah catches my eye when leaving arm-in-arm with Ant, a mischievous glint in both their eyes, and Ant gives us a nod, tipping his cowboy hat with a knowing smirk. I blush, looking into the dying orange embers that cast light on our faces amidst the darkness, and at the dull flickering lights of the tent.

'So, tell me about Christopher.' I dare to ask, 'Were you close, as kids?'

For the first time this evening, I notice his body language change. He tenses up uncomfortably.

'We have never been close. You can't get close to Christopher. Before the virus, he was in and out of prison.'

'You don't have to talk about him, if you don't want to.'

'It's fine. It's just nobody has really asked me about him before—except Justin, I suppose. Christopher is a difficult person. He is full of rage, his mum—my mum's sister—died when he was born, and his dad was an alcoholic. None of us liked his dad, but we still invited them over, every Christmas. Here, in fact, to my grandparents' farmhouse. You probably saw the sad shell that remains when we entered The Hive.'

I nod. 'So, wow, you Christmased together?'

'He hated it,' Tom spits. 'Hated being here, resented the family, resented me and my parents, and our other cousins. Even when he got out of prison, my grandparents offered him a job to come and work here, but he refused.'

'So, how did you end up in the apocalypse together?'

'Well, that's the strange thing. I continued to manage the farm with my father and look after the animals after my grandparents passed away. They went early on into the start of the virus, then when Mum and Dad died, I kind of moved in here. One day, I was out in the fields, and saw black smoke plumes rising from the house. He had only come to burn the place down.'

'He did that. To your family farm? Why?'

We sit in silence for a moment, listening to the last crack of a dying fire before Tom continues.

'He walked twenty-five miles to burn it down, and I'll never understand why. He just hated us I guess, jealously. I don't know, he's psychotic, but he was just as shocked to see me alive that day, as I was to see him. I honestly thought he would have been rotting in a prison somewhere. But like me, he was a survivor, and he isn't a stupid man. He came here because he knew that silo would be full, he knew there would be red diesel here. He apologised for burning down the farmhouse, said he was drunk. We played pretend happy families for about a week, living in our grandparents' caravan, moving other caravans up the hill, until he told me there was a couple of men he had met back in the city. He was going to find them and bring them back here. One of them had some kind of CB radio and was clever. Turns out that man was Justin.'

'So, Christopher knew Justin beforehand?'

'No, not really. They just fell upon each other after the riots, and Justin had told him he was keeping open communication with other survivors around the country. Told him where to find him if he ever needed help. Justin had already created himself a self-sustainable apartment before the water supplies even went off.'

'Of course, he did!' I laugh.

'Christopher is a collector, like a magpie, he sees something he likes, and he wants it. He has always wanted Justin, and his knowledge. Anyway, he brought him back here, and another with them, a nasty piece of work called Danny who is his second in-command... Sarah said that's who killed your dog.'

I flinch, feeling a sickness rise within me. I want to call out, *He wasn't always a nasty piece of work, he's the man I used to love*, but I don't. I just sit mute, listening to Tom's story as I stare at the floor.

'When Christopher came back with Justin and Danny, things started changing rapidly here. Justin told us about other survivors that needed help, who he had been communicating with. He told me how this farm was perfectly located to create waterpower, and solar power. How he could help me build a community, so that's what we did, and Ant was one of the first to join us. Christopher and Danny, however, started building something darker. Tinkering with motorbikes and trucks, they went out to the city, and every day came back with rucksacks full of food. Looting, scavenging, stealing from the dead or the vulnerable. Justin and Ant didn't like Christopher. Listening to him boasting about the people he had hurt in the riots, how only the strong can survive this new world, how he was going to build a race of only the strongest people, and the weak would be under his command. Things soon came to a head one night between them. A big argument. You see, they had brought back a woman. They had beat the shit out of her. Raped her, and they were laughing about it as she just lay there, half dead. Ant lost it. He picked up a shotgun and aimed it right in Christopher's face. I thought Christopher was a dead man. I didn't try to stop Ant, either. I was sickened, but you know what happened next. Christopher just laughed. Staring down the barrel of the gun, he just laughed, laughed like the psychopath he is and walked away. The next day he and Danny packed up, and began to create The Chosen, whilst me, Ant and Justin carried on here, contacting more survivors and building The Hive.'

There's a silence, as I try to piece together the information given to me by Tom. I feel sick, feel my body trembling as I try to find my voice to ask my next question. I think I already know the answer, but I need to ask.

'What happened to the girl?'

Tom smiles sadly, his voice almost a whisper.

'The girl is Sarah.'

I exhale and release a pained groan from my throat as my head spins furiously.

It was Danny.

My Danny, who beat and raped Sarah. Danny who killed Boy, it is Danny, who is the co-founder of The Chosen. The second in-command. *Didn't Christopher say there was a baby due to his second in-command?*

I scream so loudly and furiously it makes Tom jump. I stand, looking for something to hit, to tear at, to break. I pick up my mug and smash it on the floor. It shatters and breaks but it's not enough. Swaying slightly, I find the edge of a table near to us, gripping and pushing it over so it overturns. Then a chair, which I pick up and hurl across the tent. Tom rushes over to grab me, and I hit his chest repeatedly whilst I scream and sob, my heart shattering.

Eventually, I crumble exhausted to the ground, digging my nails into the compacted mud before vomiting everywhere. I don't remember anything else.

Present - The Chosen, Part One

I wake up in a bed I don't recognise, covered by a fleece blanket. There are photos pinned all over the low ceiling above my head. I spend a moment looking at them; happy family photos from camping trips, a holiday to Disneyland. I recognise Tom straight away, even though he is much younger. The photograph of two older people leaning against a tractor must be his grandparents.

I push myself up, groaning, with a throbbing pang in my head. Tom isn't here, but I can hear movement from the next room, and music. Some kind of opera. I climb out of the bed, still fully dressed, and make my way towards the sound.

'Morning. Tea or coffee?' Tom chirps when he sees me. 'I have both.'

He turns the music off. It's an old-fashioned tape player.

'That's the only tape I've found, but it's better than silence sometimes,' he explains whilst turning the kettle on.

I shuffle over to the table, feeling a little embarrassed. I know my hair will be messy, my breath toxic, and my behaviour last night questionable, but worst of all, I don't remember how I got here. My mind is blank.

'Tom,' I ask quietly, 'did we…?'

'Oh no, God no, Elle!' he splutters, embarrassed, with large, panicked eyes. 'You were pretty smashed. I slept on the sofa… I wouldn't, I mean, I wouldn't take advantage like that.' I smile. Then grimace at my pounding head.

He is flustered now. 'I have some charcoal for your headache, and some ginger if your stomach is feeling a bit worse for wear? I think mint tea is supposed to be good. Would you like some?'

'Just water, please.'

We look at each other and laugh.

'Water it is.'

Tom is needed in The Hive today, which I am glad about. He hasn't asked me about last night, or what triggered my reaction. He is only attentive, patient and kind. He asks if we can sit together again for dinner tonight, and maybe leave the blackberry wine out of the equation. Bashfully, I agree. He also asks if I'd like to choose a Hive chore. Everybody here must pitch in, one way or another, and I'm more than happy to do this. I choose laundry from the list of areas that people need help with. Aisha does the laundry by herself at the moment, and I like her. I can sit by the river with her on sunny days, scrubbing our companions' clothes and bedding. Making sure everybody stays clean and sanitary. She much prefers this job to driving the cart and says she won't do that again after our trip to The Chosen.

I tell Tom I'll start as soon as I can, and so begins my new life.

Eight weeks, eight blissful weeks go by incredibly quickly. Emma spends lots of time with Jennifer and the other kids. Together, they look after the smaller animals, gather eggs, muck them out, and even milk the cows. Her speech comes on greatly. She follows Seb around: a beautiful little four-year-old boy, and they are as thick as thieves. I can't thank Jennifer enough, and although Emma will always live with me, I have Jennifer to lean on, for everything.

I get to learn everyone's name and hear stories of their lives from before the virus. I find we have many skilled people here: bricklayers; plumbers; accountants; chefs; and of course, Justin, whose inventions, engineering wizardry and past military lifestyle enthral us all.

Ant, who is The Hive's favoured hunter, brings back all kinds of fowl, or wild animal each day for the community. Sometimes he uses one of the quad bikes to collect deer he's shot, but Tom needs as much diesel as possible for the tractors and the combine harvester. So, the main mode of transport is a horse and cart. I like this much better. Hearing the hum of the motorbikes sends chills down my spine, and harrowing thoughts of The Chosen, and now Danny.

We all spend every evening together with music, laughter, sometimes tears, and sometimes homemade alcohol. The kids put on plays, people sing or tell jokes or stories, and I reflect on my life before the virus and after, sometimes wondering if I've ever been as happy as I feel here.

My mood is joyful, peaceful, despite all the revelations about Danny. Tom never asks me about that night, and I never say anything. I guess he suspects something, but I am determined to move on and try and heal from the trauma of knowing he is alive, and a monster.

The Hive still make the two-hour journey to trade items every Friday at the allotments in my old town, which is Maggie's legacy. It has become a kind of pinnacle location for survivors to meet for miles around, and Tom decides they will never again journey to the residence of The Chosen.

If Christopher wants to trade, he will have to do so at the allotment, much to his apparent disapproval.

I also persuade Tom to bury Maggie next to Emma's mother. I know she would have appreciated that, and he does, but he won't let me come to see Maggie's grave. Not while the relationship with The Chosen is hostile, although Sarah insists, she goes, and nobody could stop her. She says it's like therapy to look men like that in the eye and know that she is stronger than they'll ever be.

I don't know how I can ever tell her about Danny and me from before, or that I know about the rape, so, I feel it best to avoid my own past, and hers, at every opportunity. Whether she and the others notice, I don't know. All I do know is, that I have grown to love Sarah immensely. She practices shooting in the woods each day with Thomas and Ant. I learn she always carries a handgun, and she and Ant are joined at the hip. When they're not killing bunnies together, they're practicing for killing people. Hard to believe she was a nurse, and Ant a warehouse manager before the virus. They are the strongest people I know, and the most in love.

To appease The Chosen, and to keep Christopher at bay, Tom, Kasper, Ant, and Sarah not only bring items to trade with other small groups and single survivors, but provide The Chosen with bags of flour, grain, vegetables, honey, eggs, and other valuable goods, in exchange for nothing more than the good faith that Christopher doesn't bring his army to annihilate The Hive.

However, tensions continue to rise.

After each trade meet, Tom returns anxious and irritated. All they demand now is Justin.

We all start to notice that on trade days, we are bringing back more weapons and bullets than ever before. For protection, Tom says every Friday when questioned by the community.

And today is a Friday.

Aisha and I have been hanging out the last bedsheets to dry. We have developed a great system, and I love being around her. She has such a sweet, gentle nature, and a wonderful outlook on life. Her family were Hindu, and I spend hours listening to her stories on her religion and perspective of life. But today I am distracted. Tom and the others have returned from this week's trade meet about five minutes ago. I watch from the riverbank; Tom disembarks at the silo and storms away to the caravans. Something is wrong.

'Do you need to go?' Aisha asks, sensing my worry as I peer like a meerkat.

'No, I'm sure it will wait, I'll finish up with you.'

'Please, go.' She tuts, wafting me away. 'Go and see if he needs you.'

I flush. It's no secret to everyone in The Hive that Tom is besotted with me. Each opportunity he gets, he picks flowers, and leaves them on my doorstep. He gazes lovingly into my eyes at dinner each night, spends every possible free minute with me when he has the chance. I like him too; in fact, I like him a lot, but I'm not ready to let myself fall in love again. Not until I truly know who I am surrendering my heart to. I thought I knew Danny.

'Thank you, Aisha,' I say, kissing her cheek as I leave.

I feel my heart thump faster the closer I get, passing the cart and seeing blood splattered on the side. The contents, all the tradeable items still there. Nothing traded. I run.

'What's happened?' I cry, knocking on his caravan door, entering before I am invited in.

Tom is standing, blood on his T-shirt and in his hair. Ant and Sarah are here too, sitting on the sofa. Sarah has red, swollen eyes, and Ant's head is buried in his hands.

'Elle!' Tom sighs.

'What's happened?'

'He's coming. For Justin.'

I look at the blood. 'Are you okay?'

'It's not mine. Christ, I think I killed someone.'

I stand dumbstruck by the door in the nervous silence.

'Have you spoken to Justin yet?'

They all shake their heads. Tom starts panicking, looking at me with pleading eyes, as though I have the answers.

'What can I do? I can't sell him down the river. I can't let Christopher just take him.'

My heart is racing, but I think we all knew it would come to this.

'Hide him. Tell him to run, Tom. When Christopher comes, tell him he's gone, tell him anything, but you can't let Christopher have him, to control him. You can't! Imagine the power he will yield with Justin's knowledge.'

Tom looks up, and nods. I see there are tears in his eyes.

'He'll kill me, for what I've done today.'

'Then, we have to fight,' I say, with more conviction than I feel. 'We have to fight him.'

Ant puts on his hat, and sighs, standing up.

'Elle is right. We need some kind of plan in place to protect everyone. Go and talk to Justin, Tom. I'll go and talk to our people.'

Sarah automatically stands to leave with Ant, and I'm alone with Tom, who starts to tremble and sob. I walk over to him and place my arms around his neck, caressing the back of his head.

'It's okay.' I try and soothe him, but he shakes his head in disagreement, speaking quietly.

'It's not okay. I killed someone, one of his own, and I'm so afraid of what he will do. He has this…this following, of crazed, sociopaths. Men like him, at his disposal, who wouldn't think twice about killing me, you, or Emma. How can we fight that, Elle?'

My blood runs cold. Now is not the right time to ask what happened, and Tom is right, but The Hive, and everything created here, is worth fighting for, and I realise I feel anger, rather than fear. I kiss his forehead gently.

'Let's get everyone safe who needs to be safe. The houses over the bridge?'

He nods. 'That's our plan.'

I squeeze his hands and stand. There's a bell in a tree, near the food tent. Apparently, it was installed as a flood warning last year. The rope is wrapped around a tree branch, so the kids don't pull it. I run out of the caravan and sprint all the way there, fumbling quickly with the rope to release it, and pull. I have no idea how long it would take The Chosen to get here, but as well as their quads and motorbikes, they are known to have a selection of army vehicles taken after the riots, and I try to calculate their location in my head, maybe an hour away in a car?

The bell rings loudly in the quiet evening summer air. Heads closest to me turn curiously, and one by one, when the bell continues to call out, the crowd gathers. Thankfully, Tom has composed himself, changed his shirt, and is walking towards me, a strained smile on his face. Jennifer is here, with Emma and Seb. Emma walks over to me, her arms outstretched, and I pick her up, kissing her hair.

Tom addresses everyone in the stark silence that follows the ringing; 'Christopher is coming. He is angry and demanding that Justin will now swear his allegiance over to The Chosen. I don't need to explain how dangerous The Chosen are. I want anyone who stays, to protect The Hive, and everyone else to find refuge in the cottages across the bridge. Keep lights off, sound to a minimum. We will try to resolve this as peacefully as possible; however, we need to take precautions.'

There's a lot of nervous mumbling, and a few questions thrown at Tom all at the same time.

'Why are they angry?'
'What's happened?'
'Shall we go, now?'

'Are we expected to fight with them?'

He raises his hands to quieten them.

'Yes, go now. Those who wish to keep safe, go to the houses, and those who wish to stay, stay, but if you do, I can't guarantee your safety. Ant and Thomas have guns, and ammunition. Please, hurry.'

There's a moment of hesitation before people start to move in the speckled hazy sunset which reaches through the trees, casting light on worried faces. I place a hand on Tom's shoulders; he still trembles.

Jennifer comes up to me. 'Elle. Are you staying, or coming with us?'

I look at Emma and feel a lump in my throat. I have no idea what will happen tonight, if they do turn up, but I need to stay with Tom and the others. I hand Emma over to her.

'Just keep her safe, okay?'

She nods, giving me a kiss on the cheek before leaving with the children. I know she'll be in safe hands.

Tom turns to me quietly. 'I think you should go with them. I don't know if I can protect you.'

'I will protect myself,' I say stubbornly. 'Let's go and find the others.'

Of the sixty-two people, there are around twenty who have stayed behind. I can't blame the others. The Hive is a collection of traumatised, gentle souls. People who want to grow vegetables in the earth, people who share the same values of making a better future world to return to. There's not many of us who have fighting spirit, and before today I would not have classed myself as a fighter either, but I have Emma and myself to protect. I feel that Maggie would have been proud of me.

Dusk approaches quickly. We walk down the meadow and see Ant, Justin, Sarah, and Thomas at the main gates, bent over some boxes. Tom waves over to them, and they look at our small collection of wannabe soldiers. People tired from a long day's work, frightened of what might come. As we near them, I see the boxes are full of weapons.

'Anyone have any previous military experience, other than Thomas?' Ant asks as we cluster around the boxes.
There's silence, except for a woman called Naomi, in her late thirties, she has a shaved head and several facial piercings.

'I was only in the Navy for four years in my twenties. But I think I can remember how to shoot.'
Another man steps forward. I haven't spoken much to him over these last few weeks, but I know he's called John.

'I've never held a firearm, but I was a police officer, we had tasers.'

Ant smiles. 'Perfect, then.'

He throws John yellow-and-black police-issue taser from the box, and we all briefly smile. John looks it over.

'Great, there's battery life,' he confirms. 'How many do you have?'

'About four or five, but I'm not sure they work through bullet-proof vests. We know The Chosen have these. We do not.'

There's a very grim silence, which seems to grow when he pulls out several different kinds of guns and quickly begins to explain how to use them, passing out handguns to those of us who have never held a weapon, and assault rifles or shotguns to those who have. We don't have enough to go around, but there are grenades and fireworks. Ant gives Kasper and Luke the job of hiding in the woods at the entrance of the farm, to watch from a distance and to use the fireworks as a distraction if needed. Justin remains silent until the end.

'I want to thank you all, for showing me how much you care for me by doing this. I feel, well, I feel responsible for you all.' He starts to choke on his words, tears forming behind his glasses. 'And I want you to hear this from me, if I go with them. You are not to try and stop me.'

'Justin!' Tom starts to argue, but Justin raises his hand to quieten him.

'Tom, this will be my decision, I will not risk any of you being hurt because of me, you understand. You use your weapons to protect yourselves, and as a precaution only, do not engage in any combat otherwise. My life is not worth any more than yours, and if he's that desperate to have his own way, then he will have to have it. I will not see bloodshed, just because of me.'

'Well, it might not just be you he wants today, Justin. I killed one of his men. He will be coming for revenge.'

Justin nods. 'Ant told me what happened at the trade meet. We will hope this is not the case; he is your cousin, and that's got to count for something, Tom.'

Tom swallows hard, nodding without conviction. There's nothing more to say. Thomas and Justin, who have the most tactical experience, show us where to stand and wait. We shut and lock the main farm gates to The Hive. I am positioned at the back of the farmhouse ruins, the building that Christopher burned down. Naomi is with me, and the aim is to make sure they do not enter the grounds of The Hive, but not to shoot, unless shot at. I grip my handgun, feeling the cold metal weight against my skin. Praying I will not have to use it.

Tom, Ant, Justin and Thomas are armed with rifles, everyone else scattered to the wind around the yard, or in the fields of The Hive. Six have been sent to hide near the cottages, to help protect the rest of our community in case things go south.

We wait.

An hour passes, maybe two, and darkness descends. We have one floodlight with a solar-charged battery pack, at the main gates, but we keep it switched off until it's needed. We are silent, using our senses to listen out for noise, but we ought not to have worried so much about that, because the unmistakable sound of fully laden trucks comes rumbling through the night air, some kind of rock music accompanying it. Thomas, our Hive protector whispers out through the darkness.

'Keep safe, everyone. They are here.'

We remain in our positions as the headlights come down the track, grotesque shadows flickering over the farmyard. I peer around the building: there are two trucks. I see Ant and Thomas raise their rifles, and someone switches our floodlight on. I glance at Naomi, and we exchange a nervous gaze as the trucks come to a halt. The music and engines stop, but the lights remain blaring into our yard. For a moment, there's no sound. Then, I hear the crunch of boots on the ground and the slam of doors as The Chosen disembark.

'Well, what the fuck is this?' Christopher chuckles loudly. 'This is no way to treat your blood relative.'

I peer around the corner again: I can see him leaning casually against the bonnet, lighting up a cigarette. There's about twenty men around him, bullet-proof vests on, like Ant said, all of them dressed in black, like soldiers. Some are wearing balaclavas, some with bandannas over their faces, each one holding a semi-automatic rifle, a real army.

'Why are you here?' Tom asks, his voice strained. 'We don't want any trouble, Chris.'

'The hell you don't! Looks the complete opposite to me, little cousin. I think we've counted about eight of you so far, that right, Dan? You got some of the little kids gunned up too, Tom? Maybe the odd cow?'

There's a wave of laughter from his men, and I whip myself back behind the brickwork when I hear Danny is there too, my pulse racing in sickening beats. I have an overwhelming urge to run up to him, to hit him and scream at him, ask him to beg for my forgiveness. To beg for Sarah's. But I push the feeling away; this is not the same Danny; this is not the man I once knew.

Christopher's voice suddenly changes. There's a dangerous ring to it. 'You know why I'm here, Tom.'

Then something happens. There's suddenly lots of movement, and the sound of guns clicking all around us. In panic, Tom and Ant whip their heads around to the darkness behind me.

Whilst Christopher has been talking, another truckload of his men must have arrived from far behind us. I would guess they came across the railway tracks, and over our fields. My stomach lurches as I wonder if they came past the cottages, and over the river. Past Emma and the ones in hiding.

Around ten of The Chosen are staring straight at us from behind the metal fence. One has his gun pointing directly at me and Naomi. For a second, I'm unsure what to do; should I point my handgun at him? I see Naomi raise her hands above her head, but she does not drop her gun, so I do the same, slowly raising my arms, my gun still gripped tightly.

'You're outgunned, outnumbered, Tom. You killed one of my men today. You think I'm going to let that slide? Open the gates.'

'I didn't want to kill him. I didn't mean to kill him, Chris! For Christ's sake, you sent him to goad us on purpose because you can't get your own way, like a fucking spoilt brat. You can't just take people because you want to!'

'Stay where you are!' Ant's voice booms suddenly through the air.

I can't see what's happening, but I guess Christopher is walking towards them.

'Tell your dog to stand down, Tom, or I give my order, and each one of your hidden little soldiers gets killed by my soldiers. Watch… DELTA-FIVE-FIRE!'

There's a rapid round of pops, and a scream from the other side of the yard, as one of The Chosen fires. We have no idea who's just been hit.

'STOP!' I hear Justin yelling. 'For God's sake. Stop it!'

'An eye for an eye,' Christopher coos. 'Put down your weapons, no one else needs to get hurt. You want to talk to me, Tom, Justin? Well, call your people off. Tell them to all come into the yard and we can have a nice chat.'

There's more movement. A clunk of metal as the gate to The Hive is opened and the rest of The Chosen file through.

Then Tom shouts out, his voice cracking. 'Put your weapons down. Do what he says. I'm so sorry, Justin.'

I want to run to Tom. Put my arms around him.

The man with the rifle pointed at us doesn't flinch as we place our guns slowly on the floor. I hear lots of footsteps as The Chosen march in through the gate and Christopher shouts at us all.

'There are twenty-six semi-automatics pointed at Tom and Co's heads. Come out of your hidey holes slowly, hands on your heads, and join your illustrious leaders.'

Naomi and I walk as demanded from the back of the house, and I see shadows of the others doing the same.

Tom, Ant, Justin and Thomas are on their knees in the middle of the farmyard. Tears track down Tom's face and I am nauseated. There's not a thing we can do. I look around at The Chosen, see Christopher smiling as he paces up and down, and then I see *him*. Danny.

He's standing, stony-faced, with a rifle pointing at us, and there's a flash of recognition as we lock eyes, and a small movement as he tenses his jaw, like he used to do when he was nervous. He looks at me for longer than he is supposed to, unable to break his stare, and then he sees Sarah. I see the tension in his jaw again. I realise at that moment, there must be some kind of feeling left in his soul. I kneel with the others, noticing there are about four of us missing. Knowing at least one is dead. Christopher stubs out his cigarette with his boot.

'Good, now we can have a serious chat. I think, maybe I've had my revenge for the mishap today. It shouldn't have reached this point, but it has. I can't let you guys think that you can just get away with killing one of us, without repercussions. We have a reputation to uphold here, and we can all agree no one else needs to die today. Okay, guys, so let's relax a little.'

Christopher walks and talks around our surrendered party who kneel in the spotlight, looking at each other or down at the floor. Every so often, Tom glances over to me, checking I am okay. Every time he does, I notice Danny tense his jaw behind him.

'On the subject of our very own MOD toff, Major General Sanderson, are we all in agreement that his time with The Hive is over? I take it you will be fully compliant and committed to helping The Chosen thrive, Justin?'

Justin says nothing. But he gives a hard stare at Christopher, who bends over grabbing his hair roughly whilst bringing his mouth close to Justin's ear.

'Let's put it this way. You will be.'

Christopher releases Justin and claps his hands, making us jump. 'Right, now the messy business is over, we will be on our way; that wasn't complicated, was it.'

Two of The Chosen soldiers step over to drag Justin up to his feet, as they begin to make their way back to the trucks. Justin throws Tom a look to say; *Let it happen. I'll be fine.*

Before they leave, I watch Danny stride across to Christopher and whisper something in his ear, looking at me briefly. I feel my stomach drop as Christopher grins.

'Oh yeah, one more thing. I nearly forgot,' he announces with smiling eyes, pointing at me. 'She's coming too.'

Tom stands up immediately, dropping his hands from his head as several guns aim back towards him.

'No, Christopher. She isn't,' he says through gritted teeth. 'You're taking Justin, that's enough.'

Christopher throws his head back and laughs.

'Tell me how this will end, Tom, if she doesn't come.'

I focus firmly on Danny's face. I know Danny. I *knew* Danny, I correct myself, but he won't hurt me, surely, he *won't* hurt me? I can't take the chance they won't hurt Tom. I stand up fiercely, facing Danny.

'It's okay, Tom.'

'Shit, the girl's got bigger balls than you, Tom!' Christopher teases.

I watch Danny closely: he glances down at the floor, he's flustered. He quickly checks himself and fixes his practiced stare on everyone but me. It builds a hot rage inside me, an anger that has been churning in the very pit of my stomach since learning who he is, and what he's done.

'What's wrong, Danny?' I spit loudly in front of everyone, slowly taking my hands off my head. 'You won't look at me? It's like you're ashamed of the man you've become.'

My nasty reproach works like I wanted: he looks directly at me and for a moment there's the Danny I knew, as the mask drops, and he stares with alarmed eyes. I glance at Sarah, taking the opportunity to stab at him again.

'Obviously, it seems the virus made you forget what the word NO means. I guess taking things that do not belong to you is what you're all about, now.'

An equally astonished gaze is returned from Sarah, but there's a hint of a smile in her eyes and that's all I needed to see.

Tom looks practically ill as I continue my rant, whilst Christopher seems to be enjoying the performance, leaning against the truck silently.

'So, c'mon, Danny!' I scream hysterically. 'Show them all what you're made of, take us against our will and show them all what a real man you are now, because you sure as hell are not the man I used to know.'

Danny lowers his rifle and storms darkly over to me. For a second, I'm scared I've gone too far and he's going to strike me, and I raise my chin in defiance, shut my eyes tight, waiting for the punch, but it doesn't come. He just stands, his face close to mine, breathing heavily, veins popping on his forehead, unsure what to do.

Tom is swaying on his spot, threatening to make a leap at Danny as guns click again all around us, the harrowing sound before bullets are released.

'Is that baby mine?' Danny hisses, eyes alight with confused anger and fear combined.

It takes me a second to understand what he is asking, then I think on…. Emma.

He thinks Emma might be his. That we had a child together.

We stare into each other's eyes, and I feel a hot tear track down my cheek as I tilt my head, replying back with my own whisper.

'She's not even mine.'

Christopher's cool voice echoes across the deathly quiet yard. He sounds furious. 'Sorry to interrupt this touching reunion, but shall we?'

He gestures for me and Danny to follow to the trucks, as the engines start, and Danny turns obediently, but I turn to Tom.

Tom, who has been nothing but kind to me; Tom, who dotes on me and Emma each day. He has his fists gripped, shaking with hopelessness, anger, and crushed pride.

Ignoring Christopher and the guns aimed at me, I run over to him, my heart racing as I embrace him, placing my lips firmly on his. I squeeze his hands whilst we kiss, fighting back tears, feeling Tom's wet cheeks on mine.

'I'm sorry, Tom, I'm so sorry. It's going to be okay; I swear. Look after Emma.'

Christopher stomps over and places a firm hand on my head, grabbing a fistful of my hair as he does, whilst tugging roughly at my scalp.

He spits on the ground before addressing Tom. 'I hope you know what it took not to fucking kill you in front of my men tonight, or this fucking bitch for embarrassing Dan like this. You owe me, Tom.'

He raises his finger, pressing it against Tom's forehead.

'You fucking owe me.'

234

Then he steps back and composes himself, and switches his personality again, chuckling like a mad man.

'They do say redheads have a fiery temper. Not sure if I've just saved you a lifetime of trouble here. Now, I don't need to tell you twice, we trade as always. Next Friday. I expect a shitload of supplies for all the grief you've given me.'

I wince and yell as he drags me backwards with him, caught in his iron grip.

Tom clenches his jaw and makes a move for his rifle, which is laid out on the floor. My eyes widen and I shake my head as much as I can. It would be a massacre. Luckily, Ant spots the same flicker of intent, stands immediately, and puts a gentle hand on Tom's shoulder, bringing him into his arms. I take one last look at my friends, their faces a mixture of pity, outrage, and fear, and I suddenly feel a hell of a lot less brave as I'm manhandled into the back of the truck.

Present - The Chosen, Part Two

The door shuts, and the vehicle moves away before I have a chance to steady myself. It's dark and crowded in the back with The Chosen soldiers, and I wail as I'm catapulted forward, slamming into several bodies, and hitting my head on a metal seat. There's laughter, then a pair of hands help me up. *Justin.*

'Are you okay?' he asks, but before I can answer, torchlight is shone into our faces, and a big guy thrusts the butt of his rifle into Justin's rib cage.

'Shut your holes and sit down,' he barks.

I scramble onto the metal bench next to Justin, and in the darkness, we hold frightened hands as the truck sways this way and that.

For the next hour, we sit in silence. Nothing to think about except every nightmare, every harrowing thought I have had about these people for the last year. The images swirling around my mind, thoughts of Saffron. I can barely believe this is happening; however, deep down, I feel there is still hope. I am not alone. I have Justin, and there is Danny. A messed-up version of Danny, but it's still him.

Eventually, we feel the truck slowing as it hits gravel, then we pause whilst large gates are opened.

We are here.

I swallow my nerves, feeling sick with anxiety as we saunter up the long driveway to the mansion. The driveway where Danny killed Boy.

I never wanted to come back here again, but here I am. The truck stops. Christopher's soldiers stand and open the doors, snarling orders for us both to remain seated as they depart. There's plenty of laughter, a release of tension outside. I lean my head onto Justin's shoulders, whispering as loud as I dare.

'Do you think we'll be okay?'

'Yeah,' he says easily, squeezing my hand, although I know it is bravado for my sake. 'Men like this are easily manipulated, don't forget that. Stay strong, Elle, it's not forever, okay. Whatever happens to you. It's not forever. I'm just so sorry I couldn't protect you.'

'It's not your fault, Justin.'

'I know, but I'm sorry anyway. Just keep your head down and don't lose hope.'

I nod. It's another ten minutes before Christopher comes to us. After most of the chatter has died down and people have made their way into the building, he stands outside the open door, finishes off another cigarette, and throws it to the ground, gesturing with his hand for us to get out of the truck. We do so tentatively, jumping onto the ground. I'm terrified. Lights from the generator blare down as Christopher chuckles, standing face-to-face with Justin.

'Finally got you here, eh, Major General? I *always* get my own way, and when I say *always*, I mean it. What I want now is for you to be compliant, because if you don't, I will go straight back to my pussy cousin and put a bullet straight between his eyes, and that will be on you. Understand?'

I see Justin tense his jaw, but he looks straight ahead and answers immediately.

'I understand, Christopher.'

Christopher nods and tilts his head, pointing at a group behind him. I see Danny is there too.

'Michael and Jay have been instructed to take good care of you, Justin. Such good care, in fact, they are going to follow you around twenty-four-seven. These guys will even go to the shitter with you, you know, to make sure you're not using parts of the U bend to make a bomb or whatever your clever brain can conjure up. BOYS!' he shouts, giving Justin a rough shove towards them.

Without another word, Justin obediently strides over to his jail guards, and together all three walk up the stone stairs into the house. Danny hangs back, gives one glance at me, and then follows. I feel my stomach drop. Without Danny, I'm left alone with Christopher. There's a cruel smile curling at the sides of his mouth as he steps closer.

'This reminds me of the last time we were alone, remember, when you called me a sadistic fuck?'

I stand statue-still, looking ahead at the doors where Danny and Justin just went, pleading for them to come back. I try to ignore his warm breath on my skin, which makes me want to vomit. In a quick action, he moves his arm and grips my face, pinning my body into the truck.

'You know what, you were right. I am a sadistic fuck, and let me give you a word of warning. Any funny shit and I *will* kill you. I will slit this pretty little neck from ear to ear and give your head back to Tom, or Dan.' He laughs. 'Whichever one wants it the most. Do you understand?'

He squeezes my face until it hurts, and I cry out.

'I said, do you understand?'

'Yes,' I splutter, tears stinging my eyes.

'Good, and don't you ever belittle Dan like that in front of his men again. You are so fucking lucky he has begged for your life tonight, because you won't believe what I wanted to do to you after that outburst.'

I cry out again as he presses down even harder, his dry fingers groping my eyeballs, feeling like they will surely pop out of their sockets. He releases me, takes a step back, looking me up and down, pure rage on his face as I clutch my throbbing face.

'Get out of my sight.'

He points to the house, and I waste no time scrambling as quickly as I can out of his way. My head is spinning, a mixture of adrenaline, terror, and dehydration. I force each foot in front of the other, not knowing where to go or what to do. I reach the top of the steps, where I sway before the doors, nauseated, looking at a blur of amused, hostile faces staring back at me. Men who have disregarded humanity, finding solace in dominating and controlling those who are weaker, just because they can.

I feel my panic rise, washing over me like volcanic waves, and the spinning gets faster, until suddenly the world goes black, and I fall.

When I open my eyes again, it is to gentle pink and orange shades of early sunrise dappled by net curtains. It takes a moment to remember what happened and where I am. My head feels sore, and I touch it briefly, feeling a crust of dried blood. I find I'm lying on a bed, propped up by several pillows, in a bright white room furnished with luxurious oak objects. Empty bookcases, a large desk, and a wardrobe. I blink a few times, dazed, and see Danny asleep on a chair facing me. His rifle is by his feet, and I notice a handgun in a holster strapped to his thigh. The bullet-proof vest and ugly 'Chosen' jacket are draped over the back of a second chair next to him, and it's just us two in the room. I spend a second analysing his face. He's thinner. Still the same thick, long eyelashes, although his hair is slightly longer than I remember, tied into messy braids, and he has more frown lines. There's also a scar I hadn't noticed before, a long-faded pink line under his chin.

As if he knows I'm looking, Danny's eyes open. I feel a rush of alarm but remain calm on the outside, remembering Justin's advice.

'What happened?' I ask. 'Did I pass out?'
His eyes are void of emotion; he nods slowly.
'You want some water?'

He stands, bending down for a bottle by his feet and throws it at me cautiously, like I'm the dangerous animal in this situation. I flip the lid and gulp the contents gratefully.

'Thank you.'

There's an awkward silence whilst he sits back down and just stares at me. I want to ask what he wants, but I'm too afraid. I humiliated him yesterday. Instead, I focus on my hands, picking away skin from around my fingernails until he talks.

'I can't believe you are alive, after all this time, you're alive and here with me.'

I look up nastily, unable to help myself.

'Imagine my disappointment, finding out that when the world went to shit, so did you.'

I watch as he inhales a furious breath, shuffling in his seat. He leans forward but then exhales again sadly, placing his hand on his face, contemplating something. He sighs.

'You have no idea what I've been through, Elle. You can't sit there and judge me. When the world went to shit, I was in the capital. I was in London. You have no idea what that was like. Not a fucking clue.'

'So, you think *what?* I had it easy?'

'Not easy, just different. I learned very quickly it is the survival of the fittest in this new world. Anything else just doesn't cut it. You are lucky you've made it this far.'

I bristle, feeling my stubborn pride rising.

'Lucky how? Lucky because men like you prowl the streets, killing and taking what they want, and I've had the common sense to have avoided you up to now?'

He grins. 'You haven't changed.'

'You have,' I spit back.

He throws me a strained smile and stands from the chair, sauntering over to the bed. I begin to feel nervous as he casually places a hand on the headboard, leaning over to me.

'That's why I'm a leader of the strongest gang in the north. I'm not just one of Christopher's soldiers, Elle. I'm a fucking predator, top of the fucking food chain. You think I'm not proud of that? That out of nothing, I've become something?' He gets angrier the closer he gets to me, and I find myself horrified, shuffling away to the other side of the bed, out of his reach.

'I am proud' He continues 'I am proud that I squash all competition like little insects, I am proud I can take what I want, when I want. This isn't a silly little game of wrong and right. This is fucking survival, Elle! If you think I'm going to be ashamed of everything I've done, or am going to do, to stay on top? Then you're mistaken.'

'Listen to yourself!' I scream at him, jumping from the bed. 'This isn't you! You are not this person, Danny!'

My heart races. I'm scared. His eyes are wild, dangerous. I've not seen this look before as he comes around the furniture towards me.

'I am, Elle, I am this person now, and if you're going to be mine, you're going to have to be taught a lesson about respect.'

I don't waste a second more, I run, but there's nowhere to go except to the en-suite. The small bathroom door is opposite the bed, slightly ajar. I can see a pale pink bathtub filled with water containers. I sprint for it, but he catches my arm.

'Danny, no!' I yell as he grapples with me.

I kick out, pushing him off, and I grab the door handle; but he's strong, and pulls me back. I hold onto the handle for dear life, gouging at his eyes like Christopher did with mine. We wrestle and grunt, until I have a moment where his wrist is by my mouth. I bite down hard. He yells, and whips his hand away instinctively, giving me a split second to shove him away and dart into the bathroom. I pull the door shut and am relieved to find there's a lock. Sliding it over quickly, I fall to my knees on the soft, carpeted floor as he starts to kick repeatedly trying to break it down, but it's a solid door, his efforts are fruitless. I am shaking violently as I crawl to the corner of the room, but I have time. Time to think what I'm going to do, how I'm going to get myself out of this. There's no window here; I'm trapped, but I must do *something*.

I will have to talk my way out. *'Men like this are easy to manipulate'* were Justin's words. So, I wait until he starts to calm down. Eventually, he does, and the thudding stops, but the silence is almost worse than the noise, I have no idea what he's doing, or if he's even still outside the door. After a while, I hedge my bets.

'Danny?' I croak. 'Please, I want to talk to you. Can we talk?'

My mind is racing, a hundred different scenarios running through my head about how this could work out.

'Danny. I'm sorry, I didn't mean to make you angry. I'm just scared. You get that, right? I mean, you pointed your gun right at me and killed my dog. You said just now you need to teach me a lesson. What lesson? Danny, I'm terrified.'

He doesn't reply. I take some deep breaths. Changing tack.

'I've been so messed up since the day I saw you. Knowing you were alive.'

Silence.

'But I get it, you thought Emma might have been yours? I understand how messed up you might have been, thinking that?'

Silence.

I found her you know; in the allotment where the trade meet ups happen. Her and the dog. Her mum had died from some kind of injury. So, I took her, named her. It's funny really, she has the same temperament Emma used to have. It just made sense to call her that.'

Still nothing. I'm trying hard to keep the shakes out of my voice. I need to get him talking to me.

'You know what? I'm twenty in a few weeks. Exactly two years to the day we first met, my eighteenth birthday. Do you remember that?'

There's a pause, but finally he takes the bait, and I clench my fists in silent victory.

'Of course I do,' he huffs back darkly through the door.

I take the opportunity to reminisce further.

'You were so attentive to me that night, and funny. I was on cloud nine, despite the virus and the lockdown. Meeting you, was everything.'

'You were naive, you still are,' he spits back venomously.

I swallow the sting of his words the best I can, trying to keep him engaged.

'You don't think what we had was worth anything? I always imagined life with you could have been great if the virus hadn't happened. I thought we had something real. You are the only man I've ever slept with; you know that? My first.'

I can hear a shuffle from behind the door. Now he knows I am not with Tom, in that way, it may work in my favour. A few minutes later, I am rewarded with a softer Danny.

'When I saw you, Elle, and realised it was you, with that baby... I have never felt anything like it. Like I was hit by a bus. You were *alive*, but you had a baby. A baby I didn't know about. Shit, she has dark hair and skin like mine. I was convinced, and it's been messing me up'.

I sigh, 'I get it'.

'Christopher told me to kill her you know. The baby. To teach you a lesson. He was pissed at you for talking shit at him in front of Saffron.'

A chill runs down my spine.

'I told him no. I recognised you, told him you were once my girl. He accepted this and instructed me to shoot the dog instead. I saved her life by killing that dog.'

For a moment we don't speak, before I dare ask.

'Would you have killed her, if you hadn't known me? And hadn't thought she was yours?'

He doesn't hesitate with his reply.

'Yes.'

I feel my heart breaking all over again, and I nod silently to myself. I don't know what the world did to Danny to turn him into this brutal, savage person, but I know he is lost. There's not a word more I can say to level with him or try to understand him. I could never understand. I must accept who he is now. Accept I am trapped in a tiny bathroom with no escape from the stranger on the other side of the door. I once again find myself wiping away tears.

'So, what now?' I ask with a wavering tone. 'What happens to me when I leave this bathroom?'

'Two choices, Elle. The hard way, or the easy way.'

'Which are?'

'Be my girl again or be forced to.'

'Forever? Be forced to live here with you, forever? That's how you'd like to live out your life, coming back to someone you are *forcing* to love you? What about Emma, will I see her again? What about my friends?'

'You mean Tom?'

Shit, he's jealous. I knew it. He's actually jealous. No matter what he says, Danny *must* still have feelings for me. I'm careful with my reply.

'Tom has been nothing but kind to me, provided me and Emma a home. I'm grateful to him, and you know what, I'm not scared of him, either. You can't love something you're afraid of, if that's what you want? Do you want me to love you again?'

There's a long pause and I feel like I finally may have pushed too many buttons, but then there's a sigh. A real, heartfelt sigh.

I hear movement and he mumbles: 'Do what you want, Elle.' Then silence for a long time.

I suddenly panic, Christopher's words repeat in my mind. *If I cause trouble, he will kill me*, and I have no doubt about that.

With a trembling hand, not knowing what fate awaits me beyond this door, I unbolt it. Willing Danny not to hurt me.

But he's not there.

Danny has left.

Present - The Chosen, Part Three

The days go by incredibly slowly, confined to this room.

It's a prison.

Danny locks the door each time he leaves, and pockets the key. He says it's for my safety as much as anything, and I believe him, but within the few short weeks I've been here, I'm crawling the walls.

I have traced every pattern in the green-and-pink wallpaper with my finger, running it along the curves and lines, noticing the gold speckles on some shapes, but not on others. I have sat inside the wardrobe for a change of scenery and rearranged the water containers in the bath into size order. I have drawn pictures in the mist from my breath on the window, and seen faces in the curtains, letting my imagination wander out of control from nothing but pure boredom. There is nothing to do, nowhere to go.

Danny does find me paper and a pencil. A little notebook where I can doodle and write things down. I end up scrawling Emma's name with love hearts a million times in all kinds of different ways. Missing her so much it hurts.

The only consolation is that Danny is subdued since the bathroom incident. I decided to stay outside the bathroom after he left, nervously pacing, awaiting his return. Even though he had left the door unlocked, I thought it was a better idea than to roam the building alone, terrified of bumping into Christopher. When he came back, I think he was surprised that I had dared to venture outside the security of the locked door.

I think he was pleased.
Even though I stood in the corner and said nothing, wrapping my arms around my body, probably looking like I wanted to be anywhere else in the world. I had pleased him by making that small gesture. He looked me up and down, undressed himself, and climbed into bed without another word. I remember seeing the scars across his body, and the burnt, melted skin warped into harrowing patterns; maybe he was right. I don't know what he went through to survive, but I do know that whatever that was, it doesn't justify the things he's done.

I'm not sure what he expected of me, but that first night (and every night since), I spent sleeping on the floor, shivering like a dog, one eye on his pile of discarded weapons. By the time the morning of that first night came, when I heard him stir, I had decided on a tactic. I forced myself to show pity for him. I told him I was sorry for everything he had suffered. That I didn't realise how hard it had been for him. Stroking his ego, making him feel like the strong man he envisions himself to be now. Most importantly, making him think that I might 'feel' for him again, that he must be patient.

It has seemingly worked.
He is pacified for now. Brings me food and water, takes out the shit bucket, and although I still sleep on the floor by choice, he has been generous enough to allow me a pillow and a blanket and leave me alone. But I know this won't last. At some point, I'm scared he will have to teach me that lesson he spoke about, to satisfy his own warped ideas of power. He says when things start changing between us, I will get more privileges. I know he wants me to come to him of my own accord, so he won't feel like the monster I've told him he is.

I keep pretending that I'm learning to love him again, and that in time, I will come around. In reality, I'm calculating the best way to escape. Fantasising about how to get both myself and Justin out of this situation.

During the days he goes out, he keeps me locked away. I have nothing to do but sit on the windowsill and stare at The Chosen going about their days. They come and go on their motorbikes and drive off in their trucks, coming back with supplies from wherever they've been assigned. Sometimes I see Justin, always shadowed by his jailers, or Christopher.

Danny doesn't tell me much, but I ask questions whenever I feel he is in the right mood. He says me they have agendas, and quotas and chores. That the commanders, around five of them from what I gather, including Danny and Christopher, meet each day and assign jobs to their men based on status, chain of command, and whoever is in favour.

There are also punishments, humiliations, and even death for traitors. They have a hanging tree, and only last week they hung a young lad for not following orders.

I think about these things a lot.
It's warped, but also so incredibly structured, in a way I didn't expect. I also know they have an array of slaves. Danny never talks about them, but I see them through the window, running around doing the mundane chores which keep The Chosen all fed, and clean.

This evening, I think it's the third week I've been here, Danny has come into the room as usual after his evening meal. He's brought me a plastic box filled with cooked chicken and carrots. It's cold, but I don't grumble or complain. I thank him. It's the only meal he gives me each day, leftovers from their communal dinner, which is a much different experience than The Hive's communal dinners by the sound of it. Music, alcohol, and all kinds of drugs. He tells me there's always a fight, or someone determined to rise above their station.

Tonight though, there's no stories or light chat, he slams the food box onto the table with a grunt. He seems irritable, and angry. I'm extremely wary of his mood swings and I'm instantly nervous.

Quietly he undresses, taking off the utility belt that houses his weapons, placing down his rifle and removing the heavy stab vest. I eat slowly, sitting down on the chair, imagining myself picking up the gun in case things go south.

'Is everything okay?' I ask quietly.

'Get me some water, so I can wash,' he barks.

I bristle at his tone, but I do what he asks. I leave my food and walk to the bathroom, where I fill the wash bowl up with water from one of the containers and bring him soap and a towel. They are still living pretty primitively in comparison to The Hive, but I guess that's why they wanted Justin so bad. He doesn't thank me, and I go to sit back down, averting my eyes when he undresses and washes himself. There's a real tension in the air. He puts on a clean T-shirt and trousers, sits on the end of the bed, and then just stares at me.

I feel that familiar prickle of fear rise. He looks directly at me, making sure I hold his gaze. He's furious.

'What's wrong?'.

'Christopher has just beaten the shit out of Justin. He's pretty fucked up. He's told me to beat the shit out of you too. You wanna know why?'

I blink, staying mute, cold blood rushing through my body. Shit. Poor Justin, *what the hell has happened?*

'Your boyfriend Tom came by today. On his own, unarmed, demanding to talk to Christopher at the gates, demanding he hand you and Justin back. He says that if we don't, they will kill six of our men, who they have ambushed and have held up at The Hive. One of them is a Chosen commander. Mark. The men here love Mark, there's a real uproar. We apparently have three days to release you and Justin. The cocky bastard just walked away. He knows Christopher won't kill Justin, but he's got some delusion, though, if he thinks he won't kill you. He's signed your death warrant, and the rest of The Hives'. He'll kill you all.'

I sit forward slowly, looking at him directly, and I put my hand on his, the first time I have voluntarily touched him since I arrived. He looks back at me, anger simpering away, and I see him. I glimpse the Danny I used to know. The baby brown eyes, the vulnerability.

He's frightened for me.

Behind all the hot air, I know he won't hurt me. He would have done unspeakable things by now if he didn't have feelings for me, if he didn't respect me. If he didn't love me.

'Let me go, Danny. If you love me. Let me go.'

Tears spring into his eyes. 'I can't do that, Elle. I can't disobey him, or what we have built here. We've done terrible things to get to this point. There's no going back. There's no way out for you.'

I am gentle, and thoughtful when I reply. Trying to keep my fear at bay, working quickly to appeal to his vulnerabilities but not make him feel weak at the same time. I squeeze his hands.

'You are right, there's no going back. You can't undo the things you've done, the same way that I can't change the last year, hiding away like a coward. Neither of us have benefited from our actions, but there's one thing we can change, Danny, and that's the future.'

He gazes at me curiously.

'Am I right to think that it's you, that has a baby on the way? Christopher had mentioned something about it the first time I came here, I have assumed that it's you?'

His face crumples before me, nostrils flaring, as a tear slips down his face. He nods, and I squeeze his hand again.

I know the baby was probably not conceived through love, and that he maybe even raped the woman who carries his child. It would no longer shock me with all I now know about him, but the other Danny, the one I used to know, loved kids.

He doted on his young twin sisters; he probably held them whilst they died in his arms. We joked about having our own kids one day, he used to tell me he wanted a full football team's worth of children running around his feet. So knowing he's now responsible for a new life coming into this world, a life he has created, *must* haunt him. He can't pretend this isn't happening to him - or the poor woman he has locked away somewhere. So, I use this as my ammunition.

'Do you want your son or daughter to grow up in this world you have designed? Because they will grow up. Emma will grow up. She is not ours Danny, but I love her like she is. She is the future of everything that was destroyed and taken from us. We have an opportunity to build this future again. Your baby's future. Have you thought about that? This woman carrying your child, have you thought about her? Her future?'

A strange groan leaves his throat, and he puts his head in his hands and begins to sob. I let him. I hope he is sobbing in regret at his actions, and although I don't feel pity for *him*, I feel pity for the man he has become.

After a few minutes, he starts to compose himself again, wiping his eyes, and stands abruptly.

I fail not to jump out of my skin.

'Jesus, Elle,' he cries out. 'I don't want to fucking hurt *you*. Fuck this. I'm going for a drink.'

He storms out through the door, and I sit motionless for a moment longer, not sure what's just happened. He's so out of sorts he's left his pile of loaded weapons on the floor.

I stare at them. Is this a test?

The day turns to night before I move from the table and pluck up the courage to creep over to his stuff, my eyes on the door, expecting him to come back at any moment. I light a candle and rifle through the utility belt, scrambling quickly for the handgun. I remember what I was taught, how to check the chamber. It's a different type of gun, but I figure it out. There are six bullets. I make sure the safety is on, stashing it down the back of my jeans, and just wait in the semi-darkness, going over a mental plan to escape.

Whilst I've been within these walls, I've been able to discover a lot of useful information. I know exactly where I am, overlooking the main entrance. I know there's some kind of guard patrol on the hour, each day and night. They start off from the stone steps and walk the outskirts of the grounds, taking a flashlight at night. It takes around twenty minutes to do the full patrol. Then, on the hour, another man does the same thing. This gives me a window of about thirty-five/forty minutes to find a way out, avoiding the front gates.

I already know I can access the back of the house through the door Sarah and I used on that first visit here. I just have to find it, then I can run.

My only dilemma is Justin.

I don't want to leave him here alone, but have no idea where he is being kept. I blow out the candle and decide to lie down on the floor, my back against the wall and my head on the pillow pretending to sleep. My heart is racing. If he comes back drunk, it must be tonight.

Finally, I get my wish.

There is the fumbled click of the door being unlocked and Danny sways into the room. He trips over his own feet, shuts the door, and locks it again, leaving the key in the lock. He wobbles over to the bathroom, and I hear him pissing in the sink. He's drunk, alright. I shut my eyes as he stumbles over to me, but instead of getting into bed, he lies down beside me on the carpet, stroking my hair. I literally hold my breath as he slurs at me.

'You were always so beautiful, Elle. I don't want to lose you.'

He bends over to my head, kissing it, and I move quickly out of his way, sitting bolt upright. My heart is hammering so hard it threatens to explode.

'I'm not yours to lose, Danny!'

'You will be,' he snorts. 'Once Mark is back, we're going to go to The Hive, and burn everything and everyone. So you will be, because there'll be no one else left.'

I can see the drink is overcoming his senses, as he babbles, placing his head on my shoulder. I stand up, throwing his body off me, and he slumps like a rag doll onto the floor. I get the gun out of my jeans and point it at him. He looks up, blinks twice, then closes his eyes. He's snoring within minutes.

My hands are shaking, but I have to get a grip of myself and go. In the moonlight that cascades through the window, I see the pencil and notebook and I decide to leave Danny a note for when he wakes.

Danny,
You don't have to be this person. You have the choice to control what happens next. If you ever <u>really</u> loved me, I beg of you to let me go. Give me time to reach The Hive. Give me time to save the people who saved me, and let us try and build a future better than this one. A future where you can be a good man again, like the man I used to love.
For our children.
Elizabeth, known as Elle.

I place the piece of paper on top of his clothes and weapons, tiptoeing to the door, and turning the key with a loud, single click. Danny doesn't stir. I feel my heart drumming in my throat as I step outside my prison slowly and onto the dark landing. It's quiet, and it's late into the night. The house smells musty, damp, and I have no idea which room is Christopher's, but I know he will be up here somewhere. The thought of bumping into him is terrifying: I'm sure he will kill me on the spot, unless I kill him first. I grip the metal of the gun harder, my hands clammy.

My eyes search the gloom. I can't see anyone, but I hear the snores and coughs from the many bunks in the downstairs hallway. *There's got to be another way downstairs,* I think.

I start to move on the bobbled carpet which is soft beneath my trainers, heading towards a narrow gallery on the opposite side. There's a door looking right at me. It can't be a bedroom. It looks different, modern-looking, like a fire door. I cross the landing half-crouched, my eyes searching for any movement from the stairs as I pass.

Nothing.

In my head, I reassure myself. *Come on, Elle, you're fine, you're okay, you're nearly there. Keep going.* Adrenaline courses through my body as I pass other doors, hearing movement and the sound of sleeping bodies. *Come on, Elle, you got this. Keep going.*

I reach the door I want and smile inwardly. There's a sign above it, hard to make out in the dark, but white letters read clear now I'm closer 'EMERGENCY EXIT'. I press as gently as I can on the bar that opens it and there's a loud, mechanical *clack* that echoes through the passageway. I freeze, horrified at the sound, but other than a couple of groans, there is still no movement. I push the door open and shut it again slowly, which thankfully doesn't make the same kind of racket.

I allow myself to breathe.

The door has led me to a purpose-built stairwell with the option of two doors at the bottom. It's not decorated here like the rest of the house, and cold stone steps head downwards, smelling of piss and smoke. I hurtle to the bottom as fast and quiet as possible. The door that leads to the outside is locked.

Shit.

I hesitate for a second, afraid of what is on the other side of my only option. *Come on, Elle.* I resume. *Keep going.*

I squeeze the handle and the door opens with a low creak out into another hallway, but by luck or chance, or pure destiny, this is the hallway I remember! The unlocked door to the outside is right along here. I swear my heartbeat is louder than my breathing as I shimmy along the deserted passage, fingers ready to flick off the safety button of my gun at a moment's notice, but there's nobody around and I try the handle: it's still unlocked.

Cool night air hits my face, and I inhale deeply. The sound of the wind rustling the trees, and distant night birds are all I can hear in the silent darkness. I see the Portaloos on the grass ahead, their plastic rooftops gleaming in the moonlight, and I make a run over the gravel towards them, looking left and right as I sprint to the safety of their shadows and out of the eyes of the house. Crouching low, I press as close as I can, and wait. This is it, my only chance at escaping.

I wait for what seems an age. Calming my thoughts, regulating my breathing. I remain still, focused, until I see torchlight bouncing up the gravel pathway. The lone patrol, on his way back, getting ready to swap over with whoever else once he reaches the front porch, and now I know there's time.

Once he passes and continues around the side of the building, I sprint, running headfirst into the dense woods and long grasses of the grounds. I have no idea what lies this way, I just know I have to reach the ground walls. With the gun still in my hand, I concentrate only on putting as much distance between me and the house as possible, a pang of guilt like lead in my stomach knowing I'm leaving Justin to the fate of Christopher, but this is survival. If I have learned nothing else so far, I have at least learned when to act.

The grass soon turns to thick vegetation; brambles, nettles and thorns all snagging at my clothes, tearing at my elbows and any exposed flesh. I stumble and trip over, arms raised high above the overgrowth, until I feel the ground change to soft, squishy mud. I'm in an area that never gets enough sunlight, a dense forest looming before me. *Think, Elle.* This could go on for miles. I need to turn left or right and try to loop back on myself. I steady my pace, turn to my right and weave in and out, cracking branches and pulling up foliage as I go.

I'm being too loud.

Any patrol guard would be able to hear this din echoing through the still night breeze and I've been walking around a long time now. Christ, I could be going round in circles for all I know, and I'm ready to burst out crying, when my foot hits brick. It's the goddamn wall which extends around the outskirts of the entire estate. I place my palms onto its cold, damp surface, trying to feel for a foothold. There's plenty. It's crumbling in places. I look up and can make out the silhouetted height, about three feet taller than me. I can see dark branches from low overhanging trees casting ominous shadows in the sky.

I have to get up there.

I try and fail, once, twice, and the third time I miss my footing completely, and come crashing back into the earth, my hand landing in the wrong place as my body falls on top of it, a shooting pain exploding in my thumb and index finger.

'Fuck!' I yell out before I can stop myself.

It hurts; I grit my teeth and wave my hand about. I think I've fractured or broken something. I sit in the dark, until the pain subsides enough for me to focus. It's going to really hurt when I try again, but what's the alternative? Stay here and be found, or stay here hidden, whilst Christopher carries out his psychotic revenge and kills everyone I love?

I catch my thoughts: *Love? Yes,* I decide, it is love. I love Tom. I also love Emma, of course, and every single one of these people who have taught me lessons I never knew I needed. I must reach them before The Chosen do!

I feel at the ground blindly with my good hand, my fingers grasping a well-sized stick that I pick up and place in my mouth, chomping down with my teeth.

This is for the pain and to prevent the noise. Standing up, I adjust my eyes back to the darkness and the height of the wall. After three: *one, two… three.*

I take a run and leap, my feet and hands scrambling quickly for footholds and things to grip. Fire burns in my afflicted hand and I bite down on the wood, ignoring the agony and breathing deeply as I push with all my strength. My elbow reaches the top of the wall, and I use this to pull myself upwards, scraping skin as I go, but I'm up! I'm teetering on the wall, and I swing my legs over until I'm straddling it. The world is strange from this height. On the other side, the overgrown woodlands have gone. The tarmacked road glistens in the moonlight instead.

    I'm free.

I waste no time lowering myself over and jumping off, my knees feeling the impact on the hard ground.

Run.

Present - Survival

I run fast, keeping to the The Chosen's' wall, making my way around to the main gates where I will be able to recognise the way back towards The Hive.

I stay low and silent, crossing over the road, keeping in the shadows and watching for any movement, then once I am out of sight of the guards on the gates, I'll be out of danger.

I sprint.

Ignoring my throbbing hand, I sprint until my lungs burn.

All I can think of is Tom and Emma, and all the people at risk at The Hive. I believe I have a few hours before Danny wakes up and raises the alarm, I cannot trust he will read my note and feel anything other than anger, so I must reach The Hive before they do, to give them warning. I guess if it takes an hour in a truck, it will take many hours on foot, and probably longer than I have ever run or walked before, but I am not deterred.

Luckily the roads between The Chosen and The Hive are quite flat. Only the weeds, abandoned vehicles and potholes to contend with, but the moon is my friend and reflects over the surfaces so I can jump and weave around those obstacles without losing pace.

Every so often, I slow to try the handle of a car, to see if it's unlocked, but I have no luck doing this and drop the idea after a while. I imagine The Chosen will have taken the fuel from each and every vehicle a long time ago anyway. As I follow the road, I realise that I'm not afraid of the dark. The dark is my friend. The dark will hide me if they chase me now.

I am afraid, however, of Christopher.

The first few hours go by without drama. I am no runner. I have never been athletic, or particularly good at exercise, but I think I'm doing okay. I reduce my speed every so often to catch my breath and hold the stitch in my side. Eventually the dark becomes the gloom, the gloom becomes the light, and a chorus as loud as any choir in a cathedral rises, the sound of the birds coming together to wake up the silent world.

Despite everything I am enduring: my broken hand; the threat of death; and discovering the first man I loved is a monster—despite all this, the sound of the birds makes me smile. I realise that sound is hope. A new dawn. There's still time, there's no sound of trucks behind me yet.

After a while though my positivity begins to falter, I have no idea how long I've been running, but the stabbing pain in my torso, and the feeling of sharp needles jabbing into my lungs, scream at me to stop.

I'm literally fighting right now against my body and mind.

After a while, I notice I've started to drag my feet in a forced slow jog, and I feel like I might vomit. I can feel blisters, rubbing the skin raw, but I'm still moving. I think about trying to find a bike in a garden or garage, but it would waste too much time. I must keep going.

Every so often, even after the sun has risen fully into the sky, I hear noises that make me frightened it's The Chosen, but it's always an animal scurrying about their business.

No motorbike whines, no rumble of trucks in the distance. I wonder if Danny has even woken? I wonder if he has given me the time I have begged for?

My body is broken, searing, every step is torture.
I have a cramp in my left calf that is pure agony, and blood has started seeping from my trainers, causing a soreness I have never felt before.

I grit my teeth whilst beads of sweat trickle into my eyes, pushing on like a woman possessed. I cry out, and at one point I'm even sick, but nothing deters me.

In the late afternoon sun, I am finally rewarded. Like the golden gates of heaven leading upwards, I see the slip road for the small section of motorway which leads to The Hive. I yell and scream out loudly.

'Come on, Elle!'

I'm in a lot of pain, with a spinning, throbbing head, but I make myself go faster as I force my feet forwards, my eyes fixated on my goal in the distance.

I raise my head to the sky and scream again, still pushing. Over the river, down the other slip road, feet pounding, muscles shaking. Up the road.

I start to slow, the aches overwhelming me, dizzy, dehydrated. This last stretch of road seems never ending, until in my blurred vision I see the turn for the long farmyard lane towards The Hive, a forest on each side. I start to cry, pure relief washing over me. I can't move any faster than lame hobbling now, as I get close to the farmyard house and the barns. I see the gate beyond is shut and I'm just about to start yelling for help, hoping that Thomas is there, when I trip.

A translucent wire has been placed between two trees, and I fall spectacularly, crashing to the ground, smashing my ankle. I scream in pain.

At the same time, an explosion of gunfire crackles all around me in a deafening whir.

I scream again, face down on the hard ground, and bring my arms above my head trying to protect myself, waiting for it to stop. I'm still clutching the gun in my hand, and when my name is shouted above the din, I don't realise I'm pointing it at my friends.

Exhaustion, pain, and disorientation have kicked in. I close my eyes; briefly aware someone is carrying me. I hear frantic shouts, then there's blackness, followed by blurred light as I try to battle unconsciousness.

I manage to fight for my voice. 'He's coming. To kill you,' I croak repeatedly, until the world goes black for the second time in my life.

I'm screaming.

Visions of Emma and Maggie's faces, blurred into flames. Everything is on fire. Then there's Christopher.

He's laughing. Hacking at my legs and arms with a machete.

'Tom!' I scream. 'Tom!'

I awake from the nightmare covered in cold sweat, looking up at the photographs on the ceiling. Sarah comes running into the little room.

'Ssh, it's okay, you're safe. You're safe.'

She embraces me. I'm disoriented and start to thrash about.

'Where's Tom? How long have I been here?' I ask frantically. Then I remember.

'They're coming, The Chosen, Christopher, he's coming with his army!'

'It's okay,' she says, stroking my forehead gently. 'We got your message. Tom is with the others, preparing. Emma is safe, everyone is safe.'

I sit back, calming down. I hurt so much, and I look at my hand and foot: they are both bandaged, clunky and throbbing.

'You are in a bit of a state,' she says, following my eyes.

'Did you actually run all that way?'

I nod bashfully. 'I don't know how. I've never run more than a mile before, let alone thirty or whatever the hell that was. What time is it?'

'A little past nine pm, you slept for a while. When you feel strong enough, we will get you to Emma, where it's safe at the houses, okay? There's no sign of them yet.'

I take a deep breath. 'It's good to see you, Sarah.'

She smiles at me, squeezing my good hand.

'You were very brave.'

The caravan door slams at that moment, and Tom enters. We hear him clattering around, sighing.

'Elle's awake, Tom!' Sarah calls, and we both smile at each other as he literally trips over his own feet in the narrow hallway to rush to my side.

'Jesus, Elle! Are you okay? I'm sorry, I'm so sorry,' he gushes, dressed from head to toe in black, like The Chosen.

He takes off an automatic rifle which is strapped over his shoulders, kneeling at my bedside like I'm dying. He replaces Sarah's hand and squeezes it.

'Did they hurt you, Elle? Please, God, don't say they hurt you!'

His face is torn with emotion, wracked with the fear and guilt that he couldn't save me that night. I feel my own eyes start to water, thinking of Danny and that first terrifying day. I shake my head.

'No, they didn't hurt me; in fact, I think Danny kept me safe, but they have hurt Justin. I couldn't help him, I had to save myself, Tom. I'm sorry.'

'Hey, none of that. Justin is a brave man, he'll be okay, we must believe he'll be okay. Right?'

I nod unconvincingly as tears fall.

'Christopher is furious. He's going to burn this place and take everything from you.'

There is a quiet pause. Tom looks bashfully over his lashes at me. 'He did take everything from me when he took you, Elle. From the first time I saw you, I think I've been in love with you.'

I feel the familiar rush of blood flush into my cheeks, knowing they will be a flaming red to match my hair. I notice at some point Sarah has left us alone, and I'm grateful for that as I squirm uncomfortably in my spot. He takes my brief movement for rejection and begins to stutter.

'It's okay if you don't feel the same way.'

But I realise I do, I am just overwhelmed with everything I've been through, everything still to come.

I smile and look into his eyes. 'But I do feel the same way Tom. I've grown to love you too'.

He releases a relieved laugh as a tear rolls down his face, and I touch his cheek softly to wipe it away. We spend a moment seeing each other properly for the first time, and then the bell begins to ring. Tom's eyes widen.

'Let's get you to safety!'

He helps me up, and I lean into him, hobbling clumsily. Everything hurts so much, and my ankle is excruciatingly painful and weak. There's the panicked rushing of shadows, and a wobbling torch light, as my eyes adjust to the darkness when Tom turns off the caravan lights and we step outside.

Sarah is there, waiting for us, and at that moment, we hear the explosions from the trip wires echoing through the night, as tyres screech to a halt.

'Tom, we have to go and get into position!' Sarah shouts.

'Go!' I reply to them both. 'Don't worry about me, I'll find somewhere to hide.'

'Not in the caravans!' Tom exclaims. 'If they get in, I'm sure they'll go to burn them first! Go quickly, to the houses!' He puts Danny's gun back into my hand and takes my face, bringing it close to his, kissing me with warm, trembling lips. I can barely bring myself to part with him, until a cascade of fireworks erupts from the woods by the farmyard.

'Go!' I yell, feeling sick.

He squeezes my hand before sprinting off.
I watch both my friends disappear into the blackness and towards hell, my legs almost buckling underneath me.

A minute or two passes, and I haven't budged, my eyes frantically searching the horizon for any movement. I know Tom and The Hive will have a plan, but I have no idea what that is, and if it will save them! I suddenly hear shouting from across the fields, and then it starts.

The hideous sound of gunfire: *pop, pop, pop.*
I stumble to the nearby oak tree; its trunk is thick, and I stand behind it, watching little spurts of light accompanied with the rapping sound of shots from all different areas of the land. It's terrifying. I grip my gun. I don't know how to help, but I need to get nearer. I have no thoughts of hiding or finding safety, only making sure my friends are safe.

Dragging my bad foot in the dusty ground behind me, I hobble quickly down to the donkey enclosure. The animals are running around the paddock, frightened to death by the noise, which is amassed primarily in the yard. I push myself unceremoniously through the gate, and limp into their little open shelter, all the way to the back. I kneel behind musty smelling hay bales, switching the safety catch off the gun.

Watching and waiting for any opportunity to help.

I've decided that if I see Christopher, I will pull the trigger. More bullets rain down around the fields of the Hive, followed by harrowing screams and shouting. It's nauseating. I realise I didn't even ask who was killed by The Chosen when Justin and I were taken; what if the screams are from more friends? What if it's Tom?

An explosion suddenly rips through the earth so loud and strong; I feel the very world shake beneath my feet as bright yellow and orange colours flash, lighting up the land for a brief second. *Was that a grenade?*

In the light I saw two silhouettes running close to the fence line, but I couldn't possibly tell if they are friend or foe. Did they throw it? Dread and terror course through my veins. I'm regretting my rash decision to come down here. I'm going to get killed.

Two fighting men suddenly crash through the stock fence and into the pen before me. Punches fly this way and that: one of them has a knife, the one wearing The Chosen jacket, its white emblem shining in the moonlight.

He slashes left and right on top of the other man. For a second, I'm frozen, still in the safety of the hay bales, but he's going to kill him, one of us.

Petrified, I pull myself up and slowly creep over, pointing the gun at the Chosen soldier. I close my eyes and fire. There's a blood-curdling yell and I don't want to open my eyes again, but I hear Kasper's surprised manic voice, as he pushes the guy off him.

'You saved my life! Give me your gun, Elle! I finish him!'

I open my eyes to see Kasper holding his hand out for the gun, and the guy I shot, rolling around on the floor, clutching his leg and howling in agony.

It's Danny.

I blink twice, momentarily stunned. Ignoring Kasper, I drop to the floor.

'Oh my God, Danny? Danny! I'm sorry, I'm so sorry!'

He looks up at me, gritting his teeth, a kind of half smile on his face. 'You made it, then?'

'Oh God, we need to stop the bleeding. Kasper, take off your shirt!'

Kasper recoils. 'You help this shit?'

Another explosion blasts near the caravans, and flames engulf the outer shells, lighting up the fields. I ignore Kasper; there's no time to explain anything to him, I just know I can't be the one who kills Danny. I can't be.

I rip the material from the arm of my long-sleeved top and wrap it tightly around his leg. It turns crimson immediately.

'Never had you for a nurse, Elle,' he jokes.

Then, there's another sound. One that makes my whole-body freeze. The sound of several gun clicks all around us. I look over my shoulder to see we are surrounded by four members of The Chosen, aiming rifles straight at us. I notice there's no longer any sound of fighting. The air has gone quiet.

'Pass me the gun, Elle. It will be okay,' Danny whispers in my ear.

My mind reels. If I surrender the gun, I'm surely signing mine and Kasper's death warrants.

'Put down your fucking weapons!' shouts one of the men. I hold my arms up in the air, the gun still clutched in my right hand. Kasper is swearing in his native language, frightened, but he raises his arms too. Danny sits up and commands his men from the ground.

'She's giving the gun to me, don't shoot.'

I whip my head back to him as he stares at me, waiting. I realise I have no choice. Lowering my arms slowly, I release the gun to Danny.

'Sir, we have the remaining combatants held up in the yard,' the soldier barks. 'Christopher's orders are to bring any survivors back for execution.'

Danny gives a sharp nod and exclaims darkly, 'Take them.'

'DANNY! NO!' I scream. 'DANNY, DON'T DO THIS!' But his stern face is set hard, as The Chosen step forward and roughly drag me off the floor.

They push both me and Kasper out of the field, and pain soars through my foot as the men scream at us. I close my eyes as Kasper starts to pray out loud in his native tongue beside me.

Danny has betrayed me.

I could have killed him and escaped, but I didn't, and we will both pay for it. I hear Danny being helped to his feet and he hobbles alongside us. We have rifles pointed at the back of our heads as we are shoved forwards, and I feel like everything is in slow motion, like a terrible nightmare.

Entering the yard, I see the carnage and gasp.

At least seven or eight dead bodies scattered in the darkness: motionless, silhouetted mounds, blood glistening around them. What remains of the big barn in the yard is on fire, and smoke spirals into the deep black sky, as orange flames lick all around. In the centre of the yard, the sickeningly familiar sight of Hive survivors, again, at the mercy of the psychopath who stands beaming when he sees me.

'Well, fuck me! More lives than a Cheshire Cat. You're in some hot shit, eh?'

He points for me and Kasper to join our friends, or what is left of them. They are kneeling in a giant circle. Wounds bleeding, dirty, tear-stained faces, awaiting death. Surrounded by a dozen angry killers.

I scan their faces as I approach. *Thank God. Tom.* He's there, a wound bleeds from his head, but he's alive. Sarah, too. She looks terrified, eyes cast on the ground. My stomach drops. I don't see Ant, or Thomas. I catch Tom's wild tormented eyes reflecting the flames. We stare distraughtly at each other.

Is this where we die?

Christopher watches Danny stumbling slowly to join his side, a trail of blood behind him.

'Shit, get that seen to. John, get the medic kit. Any others alive?'

Danny shakes his head, and Christopher responds by spitting on the floor next to Tom.

'Where's Mark, and the rest of my men, Tom? And the women and children you have in hiding?'

'Fuck you!'

Christopher raises his boot and brings it crashing into Tom's chin. He flies backwards in a mist of blood, and I have to fight with myself not to react.

'Admit defeat, Tom, and I might let you live, little cousin; then again, I'm not so sure right now. Tell me where the fuck Mark and my men are!'

Looking up from the floor, Tom spits out blood and grits his teeth.

'Fuck you.'

Before I realise what has happened, there's a bang.

I scream, along with three or four others as Luke drops to the floor. Luke, our chef. The sweetest, gentlest guy at The Hive.

Gone.

'You're a fucking monster! Tom yells. 'I'm glad your mother died before she knew what an evil fucking asshole she'd given birth to!'

Christopher seems stung for a brief moment, then in the flickering light of the fire, I'm sure I see blood rush to his face in pure rage.

'Wrong fucking answer!' he hisses, as he strides over and points his handgun at Tom's head.

'NOOO!' I scream. Then I see Christopher smile.

In a second, he changes the direction of the gun and points it at me.

My stomach drops.

There's a hatred in his eyes which hammers terror into my very soul, and I close my eyes tight, as a single, loud, thunderous blast echoes through the sky.

Screams curdle from Tom and my friends.

I brace for death.

There's a splatter of liquid that touches my face, and a single dull thud. It comes from before me, and I realise I'm not dead.

I'm not dead.

My breathing starts to become erratic as I open my eyes.

'Holy shit! What the fuck have you done?' cries a soldier's voice from behind me.

I stare in shock with everyone else at Christopher's body lying face down in a thick pool of his own blood, staring wide-eyed at me. A giant hole in his skull.

Danny stands over him stony-faced, gun still cocked and aimed. I watch Tom leap into action: he rolls from his spot, kicks out at one of The Chosen guards standing behind him, sending him flying off balance, along with a hail of bullets into the sky. He grabs a revolver from the guy's holster before he can react. Half kneeling, Tom aims the weapon at Danny, followed by rifles raised at Tom.

I have already seen the future.

I saw my future, which only a second ago I thought I would never have. A future that played in quick time in my head before a death that did not happen. So, I know I have a chance right now to change things. I scream, pushing my whole body off the floor and propel myself in front of Danny, protecting him. I stare into Tom's bewildered eyes.

'STOP! Lower your gun, Tom!' I shout, my arms outspread.

Danny adds his own command to his men. 'All of you! Lower your weapons too!'

The Chosen, primed to shoot at any second, pause, an uneasy, confused shuffle reverberating around us all.

'DANNY, WHAT THE FUCK'S GOING ON?'

I interject replying to the soldier, 'You can have Mark back, he's unhurt, along with the rest of your men. Please, just listen to Danny, lower your weapons.'

My body shakes and my voice trembles, but I stare with a steely determination. Then Danny inhales, throwing his gun to the floor first. He looks to his men with an air of authority, pointing at Christopher's body as the flames get higher from the barn, illuminating the scene before us all.

'Bloodshed, violence, fear,' he bellows. 'That's what Chris stood for. Shit, that's what I've fucking stood for since the virus, but I'm done. Christopher was willing to get you all killed, and kill all these people, for what? ... more fucking fear, and more control? You think that's fucking sustainable?' No one speaks. They are listening.

'I love you, brothers; we have survived together, but we don't need to *just* survive anymore. We can actually start to fucking rebuild. Have a future, like The Hive are trying to do. If you put your weapons down, this can be day one, for us all.'

I limp over to Tom, whose face is still contorted by rage and fear, still aiming his gun at Danny. I don't blame him, but I need Tom to trust Danny right now, as difficult as he will find it. I lightly touch the barrel with two fingers and lower his aim. He resists at first, looks at me, then takes a deep breath.

He glances at his cousin's dead body, and back towards my gaze, contemplating his next move. I put my arms around him and squeeze his body, kissing his tear-stained cheek.

I whisper, 'It's okay, drop the gun.'

He glares hard at Danny. Breathes out and releases his grip. The gun hits the floor, and Danny stares back with a relieved smile, as I hold Tom even tighter.

A few of The Chosen begin to lower their rifles.

'If I have your word, Tom, that Mark and the others will be returned safely, we will leave now, and I will send Justin back to you?'

'You have my word,' Tom replies cooly, placing his arm around me.

Danny gives a quick nod, notices a few of the men still haven't lowered their weapons, and barks at them.

'Anyone who has a problem with what just happened or is confused. Let me make it crystal fucking clear. I just killed Christopher; therefore, I am your fucking leader. Lower your weapons and head back to the trucks. Now!'

A moment's hesitation, then obediently, one by one, they do as asked, and begin to shuffle back to the trucks. When the last man has left the yard, and we hear the engines start up,

The Hive survivors get off their knees in a daze. Danny picks up his gun and returns it to his holster, giving a last glance to me and Tom, and then to Sarah.

'I've done terrible things I will regret until the day I die, and I don't ever expect forgiveness. But maybe I can help build a future that makes amends for that. If you'll allow it?'

Sarah pulls her arms across her body, looking away from him, and nods. Danny acknowledges her silent admission, turns, and hobbles back towards his men.

'What shall we do with his body?' Tom suddenly calls out.

Danny pauses. 'Burn it.'

We spend the next few days trying to sort out the carnage from the fighting. There are twenty-three dead. Both Chosen and Hive casualties alike, including poor Thomas.

We are, however, so grateful to discover Ant is alive. Knocked out cold with the back of a rifle butt, with a broken arm and broken pride, but he is found and tended to affectionately by Sarah, who doesn't leave his side.

We have four others with serious injuries. I persuade Tom to let me take a horse with Kasper, to fetch Dr Green; I can remember Maggie describing where he lives. I may even be able to persuade him to stay at The Hive. Having a doctor would be a great asset.

Tom agrees, and by the end of that very same day, I am delighted to introduce Dr Green to The Hive.
The loss of our friends is painful, and we all grieve together as a community, building a funeral pyre and standing over the mound as it burns all the dead, including animals caught in the crossfire, and of course, Christopher.

Tom is silent throughout the ceremony. I find Emma, and hug her and cry, promising never to be away from her side again. Tom releases Mark and The Chosen men they captured. They had been held up in good care in a cellar in one of the houses. Before they are let out, Tom tells them about Danny, and Christopher, and the different kind of future we all want. He's not sure Mark believes him, but says once they reach The Chosen, (making them journey on foot as a nod to me), they will find out for themselves.

A few days later, we hear the whines of a quad bike approaching. The driver doesn't get too close but drops Justin off at the top of the woodland lane before leaving again. We rush to greet him, at least a dozen of us hugging, squeezing, and crying in elation.

He has healed cuts on his face, and a purple, swollen eye and cheek bone, but he is in good health otherwise, and cries in delight at our reunion. He explains that it was Danny that drove him home, and there's a note for me.

Tom accepts I must read the note in private, and I take Emma to the big oak tree near our caravan. Sitting in the shade of its branches, with birdsong all around, I open the envelope:

Elizabeth, known as Elle
*The words I say will never right my wrongs, but I lied to you when I said I wasn't ashamed of everything I have done. I am. I am ashamed, and it took **you** to show me, remind me of who I used to be. Now it's my turn to remind my men.*
To show them they are better than the atrocities we have all committed.
I think change will be slow, but with your help, I think we can make it happen. I will need your help, though, Elle, and the

help of Tom, to work together to try and rebuild a better future for our children, like you said.

P.S. I am happy for you. I am happy you are happy with Tom. I mean this from the bottom of my heart, and I hope we can be friends again one day.
Take care,
Danny.

TWENTY YEARS AFTER

My knees press into the damp soil as I pick the last of the wildflowers. It was a great idea to plant the seeds here. Each summer they bloom, until both graves are bursting with such vibrant colours. They grow back every year like loyal friends and I'm so happy I have gathered enough to make two small bouquets from each grave. I will keep the flowers from Maggie's grave, and Emma will have the bouquet from her mother's. I wrap a deep green leaf around Emma's stem so I can tell them apart.

Warm midday air rustles the leaves in the small orchard that surrounds me. We planted eight trees here over ten years ago, and I've collected enough cooking apples to make several batches of my famous apple and berry tart. I've also uprooted some turnips, and potatoes that were missed in winter, still edible, and we have a ton of tomatoes. The allotment has changed a lot over these years, but Maggie would approve.

I guess it's kind of sad that we don't meet here anymore for trading. There are too many community groups now, so I have the allotment to myself or anyone passing who's in need.

A twig cracks behind me, breaking my concentration as I stand, rubbing the soil off my bare legs.

I always carry a gun strapped around my thigh, even when I'm wearing a dress like today, and I'm a bloody good shot, too. Over the years, however, I've learned how to assess the situation first.

I place all the flowers into my left hand, and spin around with my right-hand hovering over my holster. I look along the tree line, and instantly see the small shadow pressed up against one of the thin trunks.

'You better have an amazing reason for not being in morning school, sunshine,' I say in mock anger, with a chuckle.

George is almost eleven years old and the youngest and most energetic out of the three red-headed boys I have. Named after my father, and just as facetious. He comes gushing out of his hiding place with the biggest smile on his face, his long wild hair tied with a bobble. He picks up his pushbike and trundles over to me.

'I would have stayed, Ma, but I thought you'd need help today. Plus, it's only history and reading skills. I've told you: I'm going to be a hunter like Uncle Ant.'

'Which is fine, but it's important to learn about our past.' I frown.

George only likes the practical classes at morning school, he's like his dad. He works and learns with his hands: to a certain extent all my boys are similar in that way, but I've always had the need for them to know how it was, the mistakes we made before the virus, and what we went through during it.

I feel it's important.

When all nineteen of our communities finally came together for the first time, about fourteen years ago, we all decided it was just as important as anything else to teach the children things like reading, writing, science, and maths, but also life skills like farming, hunting, cooking, engineering, and harnessing electricity through sun, wind, and waterpower.

We also wanted to make sure our own history is recorded. Not just the history of the past world wars, or the kings and queens of the life before us, but *our history*, and how it took an extinction event to help us all discover that the way we used to live, was wrong.

Sure, when I remember my childhood, I do think fondly of the television, of transport, and of holidays on aeroplanes, but I remember technology and how sometimes it was great for mankind, but how our reliance on it made us forget our natural earthy roots, and the value of something as simple as an apple.

We all nearly didn't make it, because a lot of us didn't know how to survive with what the earth provides.

My kids can't imagine this.
They think humans must have become stupid, and the extinction event was needed to wipe away all the stupid people, but about five years ago, I made us all take the (very emotional) trip back to the village where I was raised. My home. Tom, Emma, and the boys with me.

I found my old iPhone and charger. I brought it back to The Hive. The look on their faces was priceless when we actually got it to turn on and I could show them photographs of my parents and friends. My eldest, Thomas, would never refer to my generation as stupid again, just misguided.

George packs a handful of apples into his backpack, but I have enough room in the baskets that hang from my dappled grey pony tied to the allotment gates.

I don't tell him this, though. He loves to help me. Together, we take the ride home side-by-side, slowly, chatting about the wedding, and how it's like market day, or the Day One Celebrations, or Christmas! How people from all the communities will come with gifts, and we will eat roasted pig tonight, with stew and dumplings, cheeses and breads, roasted courgettes, and spicy tomato soup. There will be music, dancing, and lots of fun. He's so excited by the time we reach The Hive.

I greet our friends at the main gate and ride my horse to the fields where our large, communal wooden gazebo sits. It has been decked out with fairy lights, candles, and flower chains. There's colourful bunting made from various materials, two hanging boars being rubbed over and preserved in salt for later, and a few smaller gazebos erected for the occasion of trading.

I mean, what's a wedding without trading?
There's a real effort gone in by all who have arrived. Already I can see little stalls of jams, honey, cloth, and soaps. I know Tom and JJ will be hoping for batteries. I see them now, coming down the hill towards me and George.

They are already dressed up, and it makes me smile to see JJ, my other son, not only with his hair brushed, but donning a clean shirt and tie, tucked into his cut-off jeans, and worn trainers; he looks great.

Tom is, of course, as handsome as ever, with silver streaks in his hair to match my own. He smiles lovingly upon seeing me and the produce I brought from the allotment.

'Fab, look at all those apples, you got loads! Will you have time to bake them and get changed before the ceremony?' he asks, striding over and frowning at my soil-stained dress.

'Yes, yes of course, if you can sort the horse. You both look very dashing, by the way!'

I kiss Tom and then JJ, on the cheek, he's as big as me now and looks away, horrified.

'Ma, c'mon. The O'Hare sisters might be watching!'

A typical fifteen-year-old. We both laugh.

'Well, sex equals babies, Justin Junior, and we don't need any of those just yet!'

His cheeks turn a deep shade of red, before he storms off. Tom grabs the reins, shaking his head whilst grinning.

'You, missus, are a trouble causer. Go on with you, and your baskets of apples, and make crumble. Don't come back until you're smelling and looking delicious!' he says, teasing me.

'I always look delicious, Tom,' I shoot back, and I know he won't argue.

I gather the baskets and take a short stroll over the wooden bridge towards our little stone house on the other side of the river. Despite what I said, there isn't much time at all, and I shout at George to get a move on as we shuffle home.

On approaching, I hear water coming from the bathroom and see a thin wisp of steam rising out of the top window.

Thomas is home!

I rush inside and place the apples on the kitchen top and run upstairs. It's been nine weeks since I've seen him, my beautiful young man.

'Don't use all the water, it hasn't rained in a month, the reservoir is pretty low!' I shout in my pretend harshest tone through the door, and then I add with a smile: 'But I can't wait to see you!'

The water is switched off immediately, and I swear I can hear him smiling as he shouts back. 'I checked the reservoir when I got home earlier.'

'But the ladder to the roof is unsafe!'

'That's why I fixed that first, and why I'm only just in the shower, I also mended the kitchen cupboard that's on the wonk.'

'You're a bloody hero,' I call, laughing.

He opens the door, a towel wrapped around his waist, wearing Tom's massive smile, with shaggy, mid-length wet hair. He opens his big arms for a cuddle. I don't care that he's dripping over the floorboards, he's my first-born and he's here. I wrap my arms around his neck and kiss his face about fifty times.

'How was it at Valiant?' I ask.

'I love it, Ma!' he gushes, dodging my last kiss. 'Aw, wow, the things you learn, and Uncle Justin, he's like a God there! He comes and does seminars for us all, just incredible to see. I'd hate to think where we'd be as a society without him!'

Valiant is a community in the midlands. *The* community. It's thriving, and very much considered the hub of all our combined communities. Kind of like our capital city. Justin moved there about eight years ago, to help build the foundations of society again, as well as setting up a school to teach people how to create all kinds of things we enjoy today, like windmills, solar generated power, composting toilets, and even law and order. It's where we all send our children when they are old enough, at eighteen, for a full year, to absorb all the information. Without learning how to harness the earth, our lives would be a lot harder, even though it's hard to say goodbye to them. It's what our world needs to continue to grow.

'Is Justin here?'

'He said he wouldn't miss it for the world. He thinks a lot about Eric, but it's you and Tom he wants to see the most.'

'It's been too long!' I say. 'Well, you'll be able to tell me all about it after the ceremony.'

I spend the next two hours baking the apples in our clay-built oven in the kitchen; all the habitable houses have these now, they are a godsend, and when I've done the crumble, and when George is ready, I send him back and forth on his bike to deliver nine large containers of the sweet, cinnamon-smelling desserts for the main food tent whilst I get ready. I rush around brushing my hair, remembering to clean my teeth with the charcoal, and I finally start to get dressed.

I have a green dress to wear. Sarah made it for me, she is an absolute whizz with a needle and thread. It has beautiful sequins embroidered in the neckline, and flower patterns all the way through. It suits me and my complexion.

When we are ready, I take Thomas' arm, and together we walk back over the bridge and towards the bustle of hundreds of people who have consumed our fields with their tents and caravans. There are even a few boats moored up at the river bankside.

This wedding has a real buzz to it, and I suppose I know why. I remember what a celebrity used to be.

I was about thirteen when I went to my first concert to see my favourite band. I remember looking up at their faces and feeling starstruck. This is what these people feel when they look at the groom, Eric. He is still only young, but the value and benefits he has brought to the many communities around the country is breathtaking.

The number of people who have turned out for the wedding is testimony to his popularity and the respect he has. I really think he will go on to do more great things, especially guided by Justin. People are even calling for him to be the first elected governor of England.

I squeeze Thomas' arm, not used to being amongst such a heavy crowd as we weave in and out towards the main gazebo. People are gathering around us and have started oohing and aahing.

The bride is here.

I turn around and see a radiant Emma on Tom's arm.

My God, she is so beautiful.

She's in a stunning white dress, with a headdress of wildflowers that contrasts beautifully against her jet-black hair and olive skin.

'Ma!' She beams, spotting me. 'And Thomas, you made it!'

'As if I wouldn't!' He grins with mock laughter, knowing he is famous for often missing family events or appointments.

Emma gives us both a quick kiss, thanking me for the wildflower bouquet. I feel tears welling in my eyes, as I look at my matching set.

'Your birth mother and Maggie would be so proud.'

She smiles. 'Hey, none of that yet, save it for the ceremony.'

I nod and leave her to the throng of well-wishers traditionally throwing grain before her feet for good luck before it starts, as Tom and I set off to find George and JJ to take our places at the front of the wooden deck, when I spot him.

Grey streaks entwined in mid-length braided black hair, tied with a black ribbon. He's wearing a smart velvet suit, and holding a small girl close to him, who I imagine is one of his daughters. Tom follows my gaze.

'Do you want me to ask him to leave?'

I inhale deeper than I intended.

'No. It's okay. I think I'd like to talk to him.'

Tom nods, and I leave a curious Thomas with his father.

We have never told the kids about The Chosen, or the atrocities committed by Danny and his men before he became the law-abiding citizen that he is today.

I smile distantly at friends as I pass but keep my sights firmly on him as I make my way over and tap him on the shoulder.

'It's been a while,' I say, making him spin around and splutter.

'Elle, shit, wow. Sorry!'

He composes himself in front of his daughter; she looks about three or four years old. The spitting image of him.

'I wasn't expecting you would come to talk to me; I mean, I hope it's okay that I'm here. I was in two minds, but Eric insisted, he's an exceptionally bright young man and I think he will do great things with the communities. Look how many people are here!'

Danny is babbling. He's nervous; it must be over ten years since I last saw him.

After The Chosen disbanded, he still had a lot of men wanting to follow him, so he put that to use, for the good of us all. Over the years, ironically, he created a fair and successful justice system. He built something amazing out of all the atrocities, and eventually Justin forgave him and joined him. Together they founded Valiant, the largest, most thriving community of us all.

Eric will take Valiant to the next level as the next generation is born, and Danny will go down in our history as one of the founding fathers of our new nation.

The band suddenly strikes up, alerting everyone that the ceremony is about to start, as Emma and Eric make their way to centre stage.

'You must be very proud of Emma,' he says, watching the blushing bride and excited groom prepare themselves.

'I am,' I answer fairly, but then I turn to face him seriously and I stare into those dark eyes I knew so well.

'But I'm also proud of us, and of you. The future we chose to make, for them.'

He swallows, overwhelmed with my forgiveness, looks briefly to the sky as he holds back tears and nods, kissing his daughter on her forehead 'Thank you, Elle.'

Our conversation is over.

'Goodbye, Danny.'

I politely push back through the crowd to retake my place with Tom, our three boys, and Emma, for her wedding day.

Looking at the little girl I found in the wet mud by her dead mother, remembering the day Danny was ordered to kill her, but killed the dog instead. Sobbing into her hair many times, knowing she saved me as much as I saved her in those early days.

I squeeze Tom's hand tightly; he squeezes mine back.

After it all, we survived.

The End

In a world and society where we are dependent on technology, and have forgotten the importance of being self-sufficient, me included. I hope this story resonates with many of you of how life could be...

Are we really living in a society where we put higher value on one's ability to use a computer, than we do to grow a potato?

I hope you enjoyed this story and thank you for reading.

Nickie

Printed in Great Britain
by Amazon